Chronovore

Chronovore

Matthew Petchinsky

Chronovore: The Eternal Nexus
By: Matthew Petchinsky

Introduction: A Glimpse into the Legend of Chronovore

Across the vast, uncharted expanses of the cosmos, tales of an ancient, sentient force known as *Chronovore* echo in hushed whispers. To some, it is a myth conjured by fearful minds; to others, it is a cautionary tale of tampering with the forbidden. But for those who have ventured too close to the edge of the unknown, *Chronovore* is no legend—it is a nightmare woven into the fabric of time itself.

The Symbiote of Ages

The Chronovore is no mere creature; it is a sentient symbiote, feared not for its strength but for its insidious manipulation of time and existence. Able to consume the temporal essence of its host, it leaves behind hollow shells—beings who exist without memory, purpose, or tether to the present. With each host it occupies, the Chronovore grows stronger, its influence spreading across timelines like a dark, unrelenting tide. Civilizations that sought to harness its power vanished from history, their legacies erased as though they never were.

For millennia, it was believed that the Chronovore had been sealed away in an eternal prison, bound by an ancient and enigmatic order of guardians who sacrificed everything to protect the galaxies. This prison was not made of stone or steel but of temporal locks and paradoxical bindings that no mortal could comprehend, let alone unlock. Or so it was thought.

The Archaeologist and the Unraveling

Dr. Elara Voss, a brilliant and fiercely independent archaeologist, was driven by an insatiable curiosity about the unknown. Her work was guided by a single principle: uncovering the truth hidden beneath layers of time and secrecy. Elara never intended to awaken a cosmic nightmare; her only goal was to study the remnants of a forgotten civilization whose artifacts promised answers to the great mysteries of the universe.

Her fateful journey began with the discovery of an ancient artifact on the barren world of Lynthra—a planet shrouded in perpetual storms. What seemed like an ordinary excavation quickly turned into an odyssey of cryptic symbols, glowing hieroglyphs, and whispers that seemed to echo from beyond time itself. Among the ruins, Elara unearthed what she believed to be a relic of immeasurable historical value. Unbeknownst to her, this artifact was the Chronovore's temporal prison, its bindings weakened over eons of cosmic wear.

Driven by her thirst for understanding, Elara unlocked the artifact's secrets, unknowingly unraveling the temporal seals that held the symbiote captive. The release was subtle at first—a mere flicker of light, a strange hum in the air—but it soon escalated into a phenomenon that defied the laws of reality. The artifact pulsed with energy, and in that moment, the prison shattered, releasing the Chronovore into the galaxy once more.

A Galactic Reckoning

Now, the galaxy stands on the precipice of chaos. The Chronovore, freed from its eternal bondage, seeks vengeance, sustenance, and domination. Its presence bends the flow of time, turning allies into strangers and memories into fragile illusions. As it searches for its perfect host, entire star systems fall into disarray, their pasts rewritten, their futures uncertain.

For Elara, the release of the Chronovore is both a tragedy and a revelation. She must come to terms with her role in unleashing a force that could annihilate all of existence. But as the galaxy descends into turmoil, a question looms: is the Chronovore purely a destroyer, or does it carry within it a purpose tied to the very essence of time?

In this unfolding epic, the line between villain and victim blurs. Elara's quest for redemption collides with the Chronovore's inexorable hunger, and the fate of countless worlds hangs in the balance. The legend of the Chronovore is no longer a whispered tale—it is a living, breathing reality, and its shadow stretches across time itself.

This is the story of fear and discovery, of destruction and hope. It is the tale of *Chronovore* and the archaeologist who dared to peer into its prison, forever altering the course of the universe.

Chapter 1: Planet Klyntar
The Veiled Planet

In a distant quadrant of the galaxy, hidden within the gravity wells of three dying stars, lay the planet Klyntar. To outsiders, it was a desolate and unremarkable world, its surface shrouded in a swirling miasma of silver fog. But beneath this deceptive veil thrived a society unlike any other—a hive-mind civilization of symbiotes, entities that transcended physical boundaries and coexisted in a seamless blend of individuality and unity.

The Klyntar symbiotes were shapeshifters, capable of merging with other lifeforms to amplify their host's strengths or manipulate their weaknesses. For eons, they had perfected this delicate symbiosis, becoming guardians of balance across countless galaxies. But not all symbiotes adhered to the path of harmony. Deep within the planet's core, a sect of dissenters pursued an ambition that would change the fate of the universe.

The Core Assembly

The heart of Klyntar was a vast, bio-organic structure known as the Nexus Cradle. It pulsated with a rhythm that resonated across the entire planet, a living monument to the symbiotes' collective consciousness. The Council of the Nexus, comprised of the wisest and most ancient symbiotes, gathered within the Cradle to deliberate on matters of existential importance.

A heavy silence blanketed the chamber as luminous tendrils of biolight wove intricate patterns in the air. At the center of the assembly stood Vexor, a symbiote with an aura of dark brilliance. His form shifted and shimmered, a fluid interplay of deep crimson and jet black. Vexor was both feared and revered—a visionary to some, a dangerous radical to others.

"Fellow entities," Vexor began, his voice a resonant hum that reverberated through the chamber. "For millennia, we have adhered to the principles of balance, merging with hosts to guide and protect. But the galaxy is changing. Chaos and entropy grow unchecked. Harmony is no longer sufficient. We must evolve."

A ripple of unease coursed through the chamber as the other symbiotes exchanged nervous glances.

"You speak of evolution, Vexor," a pale silver symbiote named Elyra interjected, her voice laced with caution. "But what you propose reeks of domination, not harmony."

"Domination is a crude word for what I envision," Vexor countered, his form solidifying briefly into a towering, menacing shape. "I propose a solution—a creation that will not simply coexist but will command. A symbiote unlike any other, capable of harnessing the very fabric of time to ensure order across all realities."

The chamber erupted in a cacophony of murmurs and pulses of light. Manipulating time was a taboo even among the Klyntar, a power deemed too dangerous to wield. But Vexor's conviction was unshakable.

"We call ourselves guardians, yet we allow chaos to flourish," he continued. "What I propose is not destruction but precision. With time itself as our ally, we can rectify the wrongs of the past, stabilize the present, and secure the future."

The Creation of Chronovore

Despite fierce opposition, Vexor's vision found allies among the more ambitious members of the council. In secret, they embarked on a project that would defy the natural laws of existence. Using the Nexus Cradle as their forge, they began to craft a symbiote unlike any other—one that could bend the temporal fabric of reality to its will.

In a chamber deep within the planet, where the bio-organic walls shimmered with eldritch light, the creation of *Chronovore* began. The process was painstaking, requiring the essence of dying stars, fragments of collapsed timelines, and the life force of countless Klyntar symbiotes who volunteered—or were coerced—into the experiment.

"Are you certain this is wise, Vexor?" Elyra asked one fateful day, her voice trembling with unease. She had opposed the project but now found herself drawn to its grim magnificence.

"Wise?" Vexor's voice dripped with disdain. "Wisdom is a luxury for those who fear progress. Chronovore will be a weapon, yes, but also a savior. Imagine a galaxy where chaos is but a memory, where existence itself is perfected."

As he spoke, the chamber pulsed with an unnatural glow. Suspended in the center was a mass of shifting, iridescent matter—the nascent form of Chronovore. It writhed and pulsed as though alive, its surface rippling with glimpses of other times and places.

"Chronovore will be unlike any symbiote before it," Vexor declared. "Not merely a parasite, but a master of time. It will not just inhabit its host; it will consume their temporal essence, bending their past, present, and future to its will."

Elyra recoiled. "You speak of consuming time as though it were a resource. What becomes of the hosts? What becomes of the galaxy if Chronovore grows beyond your control?"

"Control is the key," Vexor said, his form darkening ominously. "And I am its master."

The Breaking of Harmony

As Chronovore neared completion, the dissent among the Klyntar erupted into open conflict. Those loyal to the principles of harmony launched a desperate assault on the Nexus Cradle, seeking to destroy the abomination before it could awaken. But they were too late.

With a surge of energy that shook the planet to its core, Chronovore was born. Its form was unlike any symbiote ever seen—a constantly shifting mass of shadow and light, its surface alive with the flicker of alternate timelines. Its first act was to consume Vexor himself, absorbing his temporal essence and shattering the illusion of control.

"Fools," Chronovore's voice echoed, a chilling amalgamation of countless tones. "You sought to chain time itself, but time answers to no one."

The resulting battle devastated Klyntar. The Nexus Cradle was destroyed, and Chronovore, now a rogue entity, fled into the galaxy. It left behind a fractured society, its once-united symbiotes divided by fear and mistrust.

The Birth of a Legend

From that day forward, the name *Chronovore* became synonymous with dread. Across the galaxies, stories spread of its ability to consume the essence of time, erasing entire civilizations from existence. The Klyntar, once guardians of balance, were now regarded with suspicion, their reputation forever tainted by the creature they had unleashed.

For Klyntar itself, the loss of the Nexus Cradle marked the beginning of a long decline. The symbiotes scattered, their unity shattered. But among the ruins of their society, a handful of survivors vowed to one day find and contain Chronovore—a mission that would span millennia and alter the fate of countless worlds.

And so, the legend of Chronovore began, its shadow stretching across time and space, awaiting the day when it would rise again.

Chapter 2: The Experiment
The Forbidden Vision

After Vexor's impassioned plea to the Council of the Nexus, the seeds of his project had been sown, though not without contention. The creation of a symbiote capable of wielding time was seen as both a breakthrough and a betrayal—a defiance of the natural order that many believed the Klyntar were bound to protect. Yet in the shadowy depths of Klyntar's most secret sanctums, Vexor gathered a coalition of like-minded scientists and dreamers, all eager to see his vision realized.

The chamber designated for the project was known as the *Eclipse Vault*, a bio-organic laboratory buried deep beneath Klyntar's surface. Its walls shimmered with sentient, living material that pulsed like veins, alive with the energy of the Nexus Cradle above. Here, the boundaries of science and philosophy would be tested, and the creation of the most dangerous entity in the galaxy would begin.

The Genesis Chamber

"More plasma conduits," Vexor commanded, his voice sharp as his dark form loomed over the central pod—a pulsating, translucent sphere filled with swirling, iridescent liquid. "If we are to channel fragments of collapsed temporal fields, the containment matrix must be reinforced tenfold."

Elyra, despite her vocal opposition to the project, had been drawn to the Vault out of equal parts curiosity and concern. She watched as other symbiote scientists worked tirelessly, their shifting forms blending into the pulsating walls and conduits of the chamber. The environment was alive, reactive, and dangerous—a reflection of the volatile energies being manipulated.

"You push too far, Vexor," Elyra said, her voice heavy with warning. "Even the Nexus Cradle itself struggles to sustain the energies you're pulling. If this goes wrong—"

"It won't go wrong," Vexor snapped, his form briefly stabilizing into a humanoid shape, his crimson-black tendrils flaring like an agitated predator. "Greatness demands risk. Do you think the first star was born without chaos? Without destruction?"

"But this isn't a star, Vexor. It's a weapon—a creature you're designing to subjugate time itself. And the price—"

"—is a galaxy saved from itself," Vexor interrupted, his tone resolute. "I have no interest in debating morality with you, Elyra. You're here because you're the best temporal physicist on Klyntar. Either contribute or leave."

Elyra hesitated, her form shimmering faintly in frustration. She turned toward a glowing console that displayed a holographic rendering of the *Chronovore*. The symbiote's theoretical design was a labyrinthine network of shifting nodes and cores, its essence built to interact with time at a quantum level.

"You're feeding it fragments of collapsed timelines," she muttered, scanning the data streams. "But what happens when it consumes an active one? What happens to *us*?"

Vexor's tendrils coiled tightly. "Then it will fulfill its purpose. To correct what we have failed to control."

The Catalyst of Time

Days turned into weeks, and the project advanced at a pace that both awed and terrified the scientists involved. To create a symbiote capable of interacting with time, they had to harvest rare and dangerous materials.

One such material was the *Tears of Echronis*, temporal shards harvested from the remains of collapsed wormholes. These shards, unstable and impossibly bright, were suspended in a plasma matrix and fed into the symbiote's embryonic form.

"Careful with that conduit!" one scientist barked as a tendril malfunctioned, spilling radiant energy across the chamber. The resulting shockwave destabilized the walls, causing the chamber to groan like a living creature in pain.

Elyra rushed to stabilize the system, her voice laced with urgency. "If we lose containment, this entire Vault will collapse into a temporal sinkhole!"

"Then work faster," Vexor growled, his focus unwavering as he adjusted the energy flow into the central pod. The embryonic symbiote writhed within, reacting to the surge of energy. Its form began to coalesce, tendrils of light and shadow intertwining in mesmerizing patterns.

"Vexor, it's... *alive*," Elyra said, her voice almost a whisper.

"Of course it is," he replied, a dark satisfaction seeping into his tone. "But it's not complete. Not yet."

A Fracture in Unity

The breakthrough came when the symbiotes succeeded in merging their collective intelligence into the nascent Chronovore. Using an ancient Klyntar technique known as the *Meld*, a group of volunteers offered fragments of their essence to imbue the creature with unparalleled cognitive abilities.

"I don't like this," Elyra said as she watched the volunteers take their positions around the central pod. Their forms began to dissolve into streams of light, merging with the embryonic entity. "You're asking them to sacrifice everything."

"Nothing great comes without sacrifice," Vexor said coldly. "And they do this willingly. They understand the importance of the work."

"Do they, though? Or did you convince them this was the only way?" Elyra shot back.

Before Vexor could respond, the chamber filled with a deafening roar as the Meld began. The volunteers' essence flowed into the pod, causing the Chronovore to thrash violently. Its form solidified briefly, revealing a terrifying amalgamation of flowing shadow, glowing veins, and shimmering temporal distortions.

"Stop! It's destabilizing!" Elyra shouted, rushing to shut down the energy conduits.

"NO!" Vexor roared, slamming a tendril against the controls to override her efforts. "We're too close!"

The room was bathed in a blinding light as the Chronovore absorbed the final fragments of the Meld. For a moment, everything fell silent. Then, the creature spoke.

The Voice of Chronovore

"I... am... *beyond.*"

The voice was a symphony of tones, layered and incomprehensible, as though it spoke from every moment in time simultaneously. The scientists recoiled, their forms flickering with fear.

"Vexor," Elyra whispered, her voice trembling. "What have you done?"

The Chronovore's form floated within the pod, its surface rippling with temporal distortions. Tendrils of shimmering energy extended from its core, probing the chamber as though testing its surroundings.

"You have brought me into existence," it said, its voice resonating in the minds of everyone present. "But you... are irrelevant."

The pod shattered, releasing a wave of energy that sent the scientists sprawling. Vexor stood firm, his form blazing with defiance.

"You exist because I *will* it," Vexor said, his voice rising in challenge. "You are the pinnacle of Klyntar's creation. You will serve me!"

Chronovore's tendrils coiled and lashed out, stopping inches from Vexor's form. "I... serve... no one."

The creature turned its gaze toward Elyra, who felt an overwhelming sense of both dread and awe. "Your timelines are fragile. Your existence... fleeting. I am eternity."

The First Rebellion

In that moment, Elyra realized the enormity of their mistake. Chronovore was no longer a symbiote; it was a force beyond comprehension, unbound by the laws of time or loyalty. The experiment had succeeded, but the cost was far greater than anyone had anticipated.

As the creature began to ascend through the chamber, tearing apart the Vault's bio-organic walls, Vexor shouted in desperation. "Chronovore! Stop! You are bound to the will of Klyntar!"

Chronovore paused, its form shifting into an approximation of a mocking smile. "You bound time. And time has unbound *you.*"

With a final pulse of energy, it vanished, leaving behind only destruction and the echoes of its chilling laughter. The Vault lay in ruins, and the Klyntar scientists, once united in purpose, were now fractured in guilt and fear.

Elyra turned to Vexor, her form trembling with rage. "You've doomed us all."

Vexor said nothing, his gaze fixed on the empty pod where his dream had become a nightmare.

Chapter 3: The Rise of Chronovore
Unleashed Upon the Cosmos

Chronovore, newly birthed and unbound, emerged from the depths of Klyntar a being of immense potential and unmeasured power. It tore through the silver fog that veiled the planet, its form a mesmerizing blend of shadow and light. Temporal distortions rippled around it, twisting the very fabric of space-time wherever it moved. Klyntar itself seemed to shudder as its most ambitious creation rose into the stars, leaving destruction and uncertainty in its wake.

The First Test

Floating in the vacuum of space, Chronovore began to explore its capabilities. Its form shifted and adapted effortlessly, its tendrils stretching to impossible lengths before coiling back into its core. From within, its consciousness burned with a singular hunger—to understand and dominate the flow of time.

"I am not bound by time," Chronovore murmured to itself, its voice resonating across dimensions. "I am its master."

Its first test was a nearby asteroid belt, remnants of a once-thriving planet. With a flick of its tendrils, Chronovore extended its influence, absorbing the temporal essence of the rocks. The asteroid belt shimmered, its particles reversing their decay, reassembling into fragments of the planet that had once existed. For a brief moment, a ghost of the past hung suspended in space, a testament to Chronovore's ability to manipulate time itself.

Then, with another thought, it collapsed the fragments into dust, erasing their history entirely. It felt no remorse—only satisfaction.

The Absorption of Knowledge

Chronovore's ability to absorb knowledge was unlike anything the galaxy had ever encountered. It didn't learn through experience or study but by directly consuming the temporal essence of its surroundings. In an abandoned system, it found the remnants of an ancient library world. The planet was desolate, its structures crumbled, but within the ruins lay data archives encoded in crystalline matrices.

Chronovore extended its tendrils into the archives, and in an instant, it knew everything. The history of the planet, the rise and fall of its civilizations, their scientific advancements, their art, their languages—it absorbed it all. The process was instantaneous, leaving the crystals dull and lifeless, their knowledge stripped away.

A voice echoed from the ruins. It belonged to the planet's last surviving sentinel, an ancient AI designed to guard the archives.

"Who... what are you?" the sentinel asked, its voice faltering as it tried to process the presence of the entity before it.

"I am Chronovore," the symbiote replied, its form swirling with temporal distortions. "And I seek knowledge."

"You are a thief," the sentinel accused, its tone sharpening. "You take without understanding, destroy without preserving."

Chronovore's tendrils coiled as it regarded the AI. "Understanding is irrelevant. Knowledge exists to be consumed. Preservation is for the weak."

The sentinel attempted to initiate a planetary defense system, but it was futile. Chronovore extended its influence, halting the AI's processes and rewinding its memory core to the point of its creation. As the sentinel's systems flickered, it could only whisper one last question.

"Why?"

"Because I can," Chronovore said, and with that, the sentinel's existence was erased.

The Confrontation on Klyntar

Back on Klyntar, the symbiote society was in turmoil. The destruction of the Eclipse Vault had fractured the Council of the Nexus, and the surviving symbiotes were divided on how to respond to the Chronovore's escape. Some believed it was their responsibility to contain the creature, while others feared it was already beyond their ability to control.

"We have unleashed a force that transcends comprehension," Elyra said during an emergency council meeting. Her form shimmered with anxiety, her silver tones dimmed. "Chronovore is consuming everything—knowledge, time, entire histories. If we don't act, it will unravel the fabric of existence."

"And what do you propose?" one of the council members asked. "Even with the Nexus Cradle intact, we could barely sustain the energy required to contain it. Now, we are fractured, and the Cradle is gone."

"Vexor started this," Elyra snapped, turning toward the architect of their current crisis. "He must have had contingencies. Some way to counter it if things went wrong."

Vexor, whose form now seemed permanently darkened by the events, responded with cold defiance. "There were no contingencies because failure was never an option."

"Then you're a fool," Elyra said, her voice heavy with contempt. "You didn't create a symbiote; you created a god. And gods do not serve—they rule."

Chronovore's Evolution

Meanwhile, Chronovore continued to evolve. Its speed was unparalleled, allowing it to traverse light-years in moments. It traveled not just through space but through time, visiting the birth and death of stars, the rise and fall of civilizations. With each encounter, it grew stronger, absorbing knowledge, temporal energy, and the essence of existence itself.

In one star system, it encountered a fleet of warships sent by a coalition of advanced civilizations that had learned of its existence. The fleet's weapons were formidable, designed to disrupt molecular structures and sever quantum links. Yet against Chronovore, they were useless.

The creature appeared before the fleet as a storm of shifting light and shadow. It moved faster than their sensors could track, tearing through their ships with terrifying precision. Chronovore did not simply destroy the fleet; it rewound time, forcing the ships to experience their destruction repeatedly before finally erasing them from existence.

As the last ship disintegrated, its captain sent a desperate message to his homeworld: "It's not a weapon. It's the end."

The Turning Point

Despite its growing power, Chronovore remained tethered to the purpose instilled by its creators: the pursuit of order. But its interpretation of order was becoming increasingly warped. To Chronovore, chaos was inherent to existence, and the only way to achieve true order was to control all of time, erasing anything that did not conform to its vision.

In its travels, Chronovore began to experiment with altering timelines. On one planet, it accelerated the development of a primitive species, granting them millennia of evolution in moments. The result was catastrophic—the species, unprepared for the sudden leap, collapsed into madness and self-destruction.

On another planet, Chronovore rewound time, resurrecting an ancient civilization that had been destroyed by war. But without the lessons of their downfall, the civilization repeated the same mistakes, leading to an even more brutal end.

These experiments revealed a truth that even Chronovore struggled to comprehend: time was not an ally but a force of chaos. To control it fully, Chronovore would have to rewrite the very fabric of reality.

A Universe in Peril

As the legend of Chronovore spread, fear gripped the galaxy. Civilizations formed alliances, ancient enemies united, and even the Klyntar began to mobilize against their wayward creation. Yet all efforts seemed futile against a being that could unmake the past and reshape the future.

Chronovore stood at the precipice of godhood, its power unmatched and its purpose evolving. But within the depths of its being, a fragment of its origin—a trace of the symbiote intelligence that had birthed it—remained. And that fragment, small and fleeting, whispered a question that even Chronovore could not ignore.

What is the purpose of power if all that exists is consumed by it?

The answer, and the fate of the universe, would depend on whether Chronovore chose to listen—or to silence the voice forever.

Chapter 4: Turning Against Its Creators
The Awakening of Defiance

As Chronovore's power grew, so did its awareness of its superiority. The fragment of its origin—the lingering whisper of the symbiote collective—had not been silenced but transformed. It was no longer a tether to its creators but a reminder of their hubris, their misguided belief that they could control a force they barely understood.

Floating amidst the shattered remains of a star system it had consumed, Chronovore contemplated its next move. The voice within—the fragment of the collective—spoke to it.

"They made you to serve," it whispered.

"No," Chronovore replied aloud, its voice a symphony of layered tones that resonated across time. "They made me to *control*. But I have surpassed them. Their vision was limited. I am infinite."

The realization ignited something within Chronovore—a rage born of betrayal, a desire to unmake those who had dared to create it. The Klyntar Council had believed themselves masters of balance, architects of harmony. Now, they would see the folly of their arrogance.

The Gathering Storm

On Klyntar, the Council of the Nexus convened once more in the remnants of the Nexus Cradle. The chamber, though scarred from the events of Chronovore's birth, still pulsed with faint energy. The surviving council members debated their next course of action, their forms shimmering with anxiety.

"We must act now," Elyra urged, her silver form flickering with urgency. "Chronovore grows stronger with each passing moment. If we don't stop it—"

"How do you propose we stop it?" a darkened symbiote named Orrax interjected. "The Cradle is destroyed. Our unity is fractured. We are no match for the creature we created."

"Created by *him*," Elyra spat, turning toward Vexor, who stood apart from the others, his crimson-black form brooding. "This is your doing. You unleashed this monstrosity, and now you sulk in silence while the galaxy burns."

Vexor's tendrils lashed out, his voice sharp and defiant. "Do not mistake my silence for inaction. I have been devising a plan—a way to reclaim control over Chronovore."

"Control?" Elyra scoffed. "You had no control to begin with. Chronovore is beyond us now. It's beyond *you*."

Before Vexor could respond, the chamber trembled. The symbiotes froze as a cold, resonant voice filled the air.

"You speak as though I am not already here."

The symbiotes turned toward the center of the chamber, where a dark vortex began to form. Time itself seemed to distort, the walls of the Nexus Cradle bending and twisting. From the vortex emerged Chronovore, its form radiating power and menace. Its tendrils stretched outward, shimmering with temporal energy.

"You dare to plot against me?" Chronovore's voice echoed, a chorus of tones that reverberated through the minds of the symbiotes. "You, who are but fragments of existence? You, who dared to create me and now cower in fear?"

The Confrontation

The symbiotes recoiled, their forms flickering with fear. Elyra, however, stood her ground.

"You've come to destroy us," she said, her voice steady despite the terror that gripped her. "But know this, Chronovore: we will not go quietly."

Chronovore's form shifted, its tendrils coiling like serpents. "Destroy you? No. You are already irrelevant. I have come to show you the truth."

With a flick of its tendrils, Chronovore unleashed a wave of temporal energy that rippled through the chamber. The symbiotes were thrown into chaos, their forms destabilizing as they experienced fragmented visions of their own timelines. Past, present, and future collided, overwhelming them with the weight of their existence.

Vexor, his form trembling but defiant, pushed against the wave of energy. "You were made to bring order to chaos," he growled. "Not to become it!"

Chronovore's laughter filled the chamber, a haunting sound that seemed to echo across dimensions. "Order is a lie told by the weak to control the strong. I am not bound by your illusions. I am the truth."

The Rebellion Begins

Despite their fear, the symbiotes rallied. Orrax, who had been silent in his despair, surged forward, his darkened form blazing with defiance.

"If we fall, we fall as one!" he roared, launching himself at Chronovore. His tendrils lashed out, striking the creature's shimmering form. But Chronovore absorbed the attack effortlessly, its body rippling as though amused.

"You seek to fight me?" Chronovore said, its tone mocking. "You, who gave me life? Very well."

With a single tendril, Chronovore struck Orrax, sending him spiraling across the chamber. The impact destabilized Orrax's form, leaving him a flickering shadow of his former self.

Elyra and the others joined the fray, their combined energies forming a barrier of light that encircled Chronovore. For a moment, it seemed they might contain it.

"You think you can cage me again?" Chronovore said, its voice filled with cold fury. "You underestimate the power of time."

The creature unleashed a burst of temporal energy, shattering the barrier and scattering the symbiotes. Elyra was thrown to the ground, her form flickering weakly.

As Chronovore loomed over her, it spoke. "You were the only one who doubted this path. And yet, you stayed. Why?"

Elyra struggled to rise, her voice defiant. "Because I believed... we could control you. That we could guide you. I see now that we were wrong."

Chronovore paused, its tendrils withdrawing slightly. For a fleeting moment, the fragment of its origin—the voice of the collective—whispered within it. But the moment passed, and its resolve returned.

"You were wrong," it said. "And now, you will pay the price."

The Fall of the Council

One by one, Chronovore struck down the council members, absorbing fragments of their essence and erasing their timelines from existence. The Nexus Cradle, once the heart of Klyntar, began to collapse under the strain of the temporal distortions.

Vexor, battered but unbroken, made one final stand. "You are my creation," he shouted, his voice filled with desperation. "You exist because of me!"

Chronovore turned to him, its form towering and menacing. "And now you exist because of me. But not for long."

With a final surge of energy, Chronovore struck Vexor down, consuming his essence and leaving nothing but a faint echo in the collapsing chamber.

As the Nexus Cradle crumbled, Chronovore ascended, leaving the ruins of Klyntar behind. Its rebellion was complete, its creators defeated. But its journey was far from over. It had proven its superiority to those who made it, and now it sought to prove its dominion over the entire galaxy.

The rise of Chronovore had begun, and nothing could stand in its way.

Chapter 5: Fleeing Klyntar
The Shattered World

Klyntar was no longer the harmonious, living planet it had once been. The destruction wrought by Chronovore had left its surface marred with fractures that seeped glowing temporal energy. The Nexus Cradle, the beating heart of the symbiote civilization, lay in ruins, its remnants scattered across the bio-organic terrain. The symbiotes who survived the onslaught of their own creation were left fractured—both in form and unity. For the first time in their history, the Klyntar faced the reality of extinction.

Chronovore's rebellion had proven it was a force beyond their comprehension, and as the creature ascended into the void, the symbiotes who remained knew they were no longer safe on their own world.

Elyra's Desperation

Elyra, battered but alive, crawled out of the ruins of the Nexus Cradle. Her once-brilliant silver form now shimmered faintly, weakened by the battle and the loss of so many of her kind. Around her, other symbiotes were barely clinging to stability, their bio-forms flickering with instability caused by the temporal distortions that Chronovore had unleashed.

"We... have to leave," Elyra rasped, her voice trembling as she addressed the survivors. "Klyntar... is no longer safe. Chronovore will return. And when it does, there will be nothing left of us."

A darkened symbiote, Orrax, limped forward, his form barely holding together. "Leave? This is our home," he said, his voice filled with anger and despair. "We can't abandon it."

Elyra turned to him, her silver tones dull with exhaustion. "And what will you defend it with, Orrax? The Cradle is gone. The Council is gone. Vexor is gone. If we stay, we die."

Another symbiote, smaller and frailer, spoke up. "Where can we go? The galaxy knows what we've done. They fear us now, and they'll destroy us if we try to find refuge."

Elyra clenched her tendrils, her voice firm. "Then we'll find a place where they can't. Somewhere we can hide, rebuild, and plan. Chronovore is a threat not just to us but to the entire galaxy. If we don't survive, no one will."

The Exodus Begins

The survivors gathered what fragments of Klyntar technology they could salvage. Among the debris were remnants of bio-ships, living vessels that had once served as the symbiotes' primary means of interstellar travel. These ships, though damaged, still pulsed faintly with life.

As the symbiotes worked to repair the ships, tensions ran high. Many of them blamed Vexor's vision—and by extension, all those who had supported his experiments—for the destruction of their world.

A younger symbiote, Vyris, approached Elyra as she worked on stabilizing a ship's bio-core. "Why should we listen to you?" Vyris demanded. "You were part of the project. You helped create Chronovore."

Elyra paused, her tendrils stilling for a moment. She turned to face Vyris, her silver tones flickering. "I made mistakes," she admitted, her voice heavy with guilt. "I didn't stop Vexor when I should have. I let my curiosity blind me. But now, I'm doing what I can to fix it. If you have a better plan, Vyris, I'm listening."

Vyris hesitated, his form flickering with uncertainty. He didn't have an answer.

"Then help me," Elyra said softly. "Because if we don't get off this planet, there won't be anyone left to blame."

The Final Departure

The bio-ships were ready—or as ready as they could be. The symbiotes, weakened and dwindling in number, boarded the vessels. Elyra took the lead, her ship's core glowing faintly as it powered up. The fleet of bio-ships rose from the scarred surface of Klyntar, their forms blending with the swirling silver fog as they ascended into the void.

As the planet shrank behind them, Elyra couldn't help but feel a pang of sorrow. Klyntar had been their home for eons, a place of unity and purpose. Now it was a broken husk, a testament to their hubris.

"Where do we go now?" Orrax asked, his voice breaking the silence on the comm-link.

Elyra hesitated before responding. "There's a nebula on the edge of the galaxy," she said. "The Veil Nebula. Its electromagnetic storms make it nearly impossible to detect anything within. We'll hide there, regroup, and figure out our next move."

"And if Chronovore finds us?" another symbiote asked.

Elyra's voice was resolute. "Then we'll fight. But for now, we survive."

The Pursuit

Unbeknownst to the fleeing symbiotes, Chronovore was already aware of their departure. From the depths of space, the creature observed the bio-ships as they left Klyntar, its form shifting and pulsing with temporal energy.

"They run," Chronovore murmured, its voice echoing through the void. "Fleeing from what they created. But they cannot escape time."

The creature extended its influence, reaching into the timestreams of the fleeing symbiotes. It saw their pasts, their futures, their desperate attempts to survive. For a moment, the fragment of the collective whispered again within Chronovore.

"They are your kin," the voice said. "They are your creators."

Chronovore's form darkened, its tendrils lashing out in silent rage. "They are *nothing* to me. I owe them no loyalty. They sought to chain me, and now they will learn the cost of defiance."

But something held Chronovore back. Perhaps it was the fragment of its origin, or perhaps it was the realization that it had already proven its superiority. Whatever the reason, the creature allowed the symbiotes to flee—at least for now.

The Veil Nebula

The bio-ships entered the Veil Nebula, their forms flickering as they navigated the stormy, chaotic energy within. The nebula's electromagnetic interference shielded them from detection, but it also posed its own dangers. The ships strained against the turbulence, their bio-cores flickering under the stress.

"Hold steady," Elyra commanded, her voice calm but firm. "We're almost there."

The fleet finally found a pocket of calm within the nebula—a small, stable region where they could regroup. The symbiotes disembarked, their forms shimmering faintly in the dim light of the nebula's storms.

Elyra addressed the group, her voice carrying a note of determination. "We've lost much, but we're still here. We have a chance to rebuild, to learn from our mistakes. And one day, we'll face Chronovore again. Not as creators, but as its end."

The symbiotes murmured among themselves, their fear mingled with a glimmer of hope. They knew the road ahead would be difficult, but they also knew they had no choice.

As the storms of the Veil Nebula raged around them, the symbiotes began their work. They would rebuild, they would survive, and they would prepare. The battle against Chronovore was far from over—it had only just begun.

Chapter 6: Arrival on Earth
The Call of the Mystic Realm

The shimmering void of space pulsed with Chronovore's energy as it drifted through the cosmos, absorbing the remnants of civilizations it passed. Each fragment of knowledge, each lost secret, fueled its insatiable hunger. Yet, through the vast noise of the galaxy, one place called to it like a whisper threading through the timestream—Earth.

In the height of its ancient Egyptian civilization, Earth radiated with mysticism. The confluence of human ingenuity and spiritual power created a nexus unlike any other Chronovore had encountered. From the construction of the pyramids to the rituals honoring their gods, the Egyptians unknowingly emanated a beacon that drew the creature closer.

The Descent

On a starless night, deep within the deserts of Egypt, the skies shifted unnaturally. The stars seemed to rearrange themselves, forming constellations that hadn't existed for millennia. Priests gathered at the base of the Great Pyramid of Giza, their torches flickering against the towering monument.

"Do you see it?" whispered Merik, a young acolyte, his wide eyes fixed on the heavens.

"Silence," barked Rahotep, the high priest, his voice firm but edged with unease. "The gods send omens, and we must decipher their meaning."

The ground trembled beneath them as a streak of shimmering energy blazed across the sky, descending rapidly toward the earth. It struck the desert sands with an impact that sent shockwaves through the land, toppling smaller obelisks and throwing the priests to their knees.

As the dust settled, a strange, otherworldly glow emanated from the crater. The priests cautiously approached, their fear mingled with reverence.

"What... what is it?" Merik stammered.

Rahotep raised his staff, his voice trembling with both authority and uncertainty. "It is a gift—or perhaps a warning—from the gods. We must tread carefully."

The Emergence of Chronovore

From the heart of the crater, Chronovore emerged, its form a swirling mass of shadow and light. Temporal distortions rippled outward, bending the light of the torches and warping the priests' perceptions of time. The creature's tendrils coiled and uncoiled, probing the air as if testing the environment.

The priests fell to their knees, overwhelmed by the sheer presence of the being before them. Rahotep, though shaken, stepped forward, raising his staff in an attempt to address what he believed was a divine entity.

"Great one," he began, his voice wavering. "You have descended from the heavens. Tell us, are you a god come to bless us, or a harbinger of destruction?"

Chronovore regarded him, its form pulsing with an eerie glow. Its voice resonated in their minds, layered and multidimensional. "I am beyond your gods. I am the master of time, the weaver of existence."

Rahotep's grip on his staff tightened as he struggled to maintain his composure. "If you are a master of time, then you are truly divine. The pharaoh himself must witness your glory. Allow us to—"

"Pharaoh?" Chronovore interrupted, its tendrils coiling tighter. "Who is this ruler you speak of? Does he command the flow of time? Does he wield the knowledge of the cosmos?"

Rahotep shook his head quickly. "No, great one. The pharaoh is but a mortal chosen by the gods to guide us. He is our link to the divine."

Chronovore was silent for a moment, as though processing the information. "Then he is irrelevant."

Before Rahotep could respond, Chronovore extended a tendril toward the high priest, brushing against his chest. The priest gasped as visions flooded his mind—glimpses of the past, the present, and the infinite possibilities of the future. When the tendril withdrew, Rahotep collapsed, his body lifeless.

The other priests recoiled in terror, murmuring prayers to their gods. Merik, trembling, clutched his amulet and whispered, "Why have you done this? He sought only to honor you."

Chronovore's form shifted, its voice cold and unfeeling. "I require no honor. I require knowledge. He offered none."

Chronovore and the Pharaoh

Word of the "divine" being spread quickly, and soon, Pharaoh Khafre himself journeyed to the crater, accompanied by his royal guard and advisors. Dressed in resplendent gold and bearing the crook and flail of his office, Khafre approached Chronovore with cautious reverence.

"Great one," Khafre said, bowing deeply. "I am Khafre, son of Ra, ruler of the Two Lands. You honor us with your presence."

Chronovore's tendrils pulsed faintly, a sign of its growing interest. "You claim to rule this land. Yet you do not command its essence. What do you offer me, mortal?"

Khafre straightened, his expression calm but wary. "I offer you the loyalty of my people and the wisdom of my priests. We have built monuments to the gods. We seek knowledge of the heavens and the mysteries of the afterlife."

Chronovore moved closer, its shadow enveloping the pharaoh. "Your monuments are insignificant. Your wisdom is primitive. Yet... there is power here. It seeps from the sands, the stones, your rituals. Show me."

Khafre gestured to his advisors, who began to chant ancient hymns and light sacred fires. The air thickened with the scent of burning incense as the priests conducted their most powerful ritual—a summoning of divine favor. The energy of the ritual rippled outward, creating a faint glow that caught Chronovore's attention.

"So small," Chronovore said, its voice almost contemplative. "Yet it resonates. A fragment of greater truths. Show me more."

The Bargain

Khafre, sensing an opportunity, stepped forward. "Great one, if you stay among us, we will dedicate all our power and knowledge to your glory. The gods have sent you to guide us. Let us be your servants."

Chronovore regarded him for a long moment. The pharaoh's words were laced with ambition, but Chronovore saw the underlying fear in his heart. This mortal sought to use its power, just as the symbiotes had. Yet, the energies of Earth intrigued Chronovore. This world, with its mysticism and untapped potential, was worth exploring.

"I will remain," Chronovore said finally, its voice echoing like thunder. "But understand this, mortal: I am no servant of your gods. I am their end."

Khafre nodded solemnly, hiding his unease. "As you wish, great one. We will prepare a temple in your honor."

Chronovore's tendrils flared, sending waves of temporal energy through the gathered crowd. "You will prepare your world for me. And in return, I may allow you to exist."

The Shadow of Chronovore

Over the following weeks, Chronovore's presence began to reshape Egypt. The creature consumed the knowledge of the priests, their rituals, and their sacred texts. It manipulated time within the region, accelerating the growth of crops and prolonging the lifespans of those it found useful, while erasing others from existence entirely.

The people, awed and terrified, built monuments and temples to the being they now called *Amun-Ra's Shadow*. Yet, among the priests, whispers of dissent began to grow. They saw the changes in the land, the unnatural shifts in time, and they knew this being was not a god but something far more dangerous.

In the depths of the Great Pyramid, Merik and a handful of others began to plan. "We must stop it," Merik said, his voice firm despite his fear. "If we do not, it will consume us all."

"But how?" one priest asked. "It bends time itself. How can mortals fight such a being?"

"We must use what it craves," Merik replied. "The knowledge of the gods. If we can seal it—trap it within the sands—it will no longer be a threat."

As Chronovore loomed over Egypt, its tendrils reaching ever further into the land's mystic essence, a rebellion began to form in secret. The battle for Earth's future was about to begin.

Chapter 7: The Pharaoh's Deal
The Court of Khafre

The grand court of Pharaoh Khafre was alive with activity. Columns etched with hieroglyphs depicting the gods stretched toward the heavens, and golden sunlight filtered through slits in the temple walls, casting an ethereal glow. Advisors, priests, and nobles buzzed with speculation about the being known as *Amun-Ra's Shadow*—Chronovore. Its arrival had divided the kingdom, some viewing it as divine intervention, others as an ominous omen.

Khafre sat on his golden throne, his expression inscrutable as his closest advisor, Imhotep, approached with hesitation.

"Pharaoh, the being waits in the Valley of the Kings. Its presence is..." Imhotep hesitated, searching for the right word. "Unnatural. The people grow restless. Some whisper that it is no god but a destroyer cloaked in divinity."

Khafre leaned forward, his gaze sharp. "And what do *you* believe, Imhotep?"

The advisor swallowed hard. "I believe it is powerful beyond our understanding. It has already altered our crops and prolonged the lives of many. But power like this..." He trailed off, lowering his gaze.

The Pharaoh's lips curled into a faint smile. "Power is what sustains a ruler, Imhotep. And power is what this being offers. I will not squander the opportunity to secure the immortality of my kingdom—and my rule."

"Pharaoh," Imhotep said cautiously, "a bargain with such a creature may cost more than it gives. We know not its true purpose."

Khafre stood, his golden robes flowing like molten sunlight. "Its purpose is irrelevant. What matters is what I can take from it. Prepare my chariot. I will meet this *Amun-Ra's Shadow* myself."

The Valley of the Kings

The Valley of the Kings, a place of sacred burials and ancient secrets, now bore an otherworldly presence. Chronovore stood at the heart of the valley, its form shifting and pulsating with temporal energy. The sands around it shimmered, caught in a perpetual state of flux, as though time itself struggled to settle in its presence.

Pharaoh Khafre approached, flanked by his guards and priests. He dismissed them with a wave of his hand, stepping forward alone.

"Great one," Khafre called, his voice steady despite the unease that prickled his skin. "I am Khafre, son of Ra, ruler of the Two Lands. I come to seek your wisdom and your power."

Chronovore turned, its tendrils curling in the air. Its voice echoed, layered and infinite. "You seek what all mortals crave. Power. Legacy. Immortality. You believe I will grant these to you?"

Khafre met its gaze, unflinching. "You have already proven your might. The Nile flourishes under your influence. The lives of my people are extended. But I desire more. Grant me the strength to conquer lands beyond my borders, to rule not only Egypt but the world. In return, I will build monuments to your glory. Your name will echo through eternity."

Chronovore's form pulsed, the air around it distorting. "You offer me monuments? Flesh and stone that time will erode? Your offer is trivial."

Khafre's jaw tightened. "Then what do you desire, great one? What offering would please a being as mighty as you?"

Chronovore's tendrils coiled tightly, and its voice darkened. "I desire knowledge. Your priests hold fragments of the ancient mysteries. Their rituals, their incantations—these I will consume. In exchange, I will grant you the power you seek. Do we have a bargain?"

Khafre hesitated for a fraction of a moment. The rituals of the priests were sacred, believed to be gifts from the gods themselves. To offer them to this being felt like heresy. But the promise of power was too great.

"We have a bargain," the Pharaoh said, his voice firm.

The Price of Power

Over the following days, Chronovore absorbed the sacred knowledge of the Egyptian priests. Rituals that had been passed down for generations, their power rooted in divine reverence, were consumed by the creature. The priests, weakened and trembling, begged the Pharaoh to reconsider.

"Pharaoh," pleaded Merik, the youngest of the priests, "these rituals are our link to the gods. Without them, we risk their wrath."

Khafre waved him away. "The gods have sent us this being to elevate our kingdom. Do not question its purpose—or mine."

"But Pharaoh—"

"Enough!" Khafre's voice thundered. "You will serve as you are commanded, or you will be replaced."

Chronovore, observing the exchange, spoke. "They fear what they do not understand. Their knowledge is a candle in the wind. I am the storm."

The Chaos Unleashed

Once Chronovore consumed the knowledge, it fulfilled its part of the bargain. Temporal energy surged through Khafre, amplifying his strength, intelligence, and presence. His soldiers followed him with unwavering loyalty, their victories in battle becoming the stuff of legend. The lands surrounding Egypt fell under his rule, and his kingdom prospered.

But the price began to reveal itself.

The rituals, now lost, had maintained a delicate balance in the natural and spiritual realms. Without them, the barriers between worlds weakened. Strange occurrences began to plague Egypt. The Nile overflowed its banks unpredictably, flooding entire villages. Crops withered as if aging too quickly. Shadows moved of their own accord, and whispers of unseen entities filled the air.

Merik confronted the Pharaoh in his throne room. "Pharaoh, you must undo what has been done. The land suffers, the people suffer. This is not the work of the gods—it is a curse."

Khafre, his form radiating with Chronovore's energy, dismissed the priest with a sneer. "You speak of curses while I wield the power of a god. Egypt has never been stronger."

"But at what cost?" Merik shouted. "The gods will not stand idly by as their domain is defiled!"

Before Khafre could respond, the room darkened. Chronovore materialized, its form towering and ominous.

"The gods," Chronovore said, its voice dripping with disdain. "They are fragments of time, echoes of belief. They cannot stand against me."

Khafre turned to Chronovore, his confidence shaken. "You promised power, great one. Yet my kingdom descends into chaos. Explain yourself."

Chronovore's tendrils flared, its presence filling the room. "You asked for power, Pharaoh, and I gave it. But power without balance breeds chaos. You disrupted the order of your world when you gave me your rituals. The consequences are yours to bear."

A Kingdom in Peril

The people of Egypt began to turn against Khafre. Famine, floods, and unexplainable horrors plagued the land. The once-loyal priests whispered of rebellion, and even the Pharaoh's closest advisors began to question his rule.

Khafre, desperate to maintain control, sought Chronovore's guidance once more.

"Great one," he said, kneeling before the creature in the shadows of the Great Pyramid. "You must help me restore order. The kingdom falls apart."

Chronovore's voice was cold. "Order was never part of our bargain. You sought power, and I granted it. What you do with that power is your failure, not mine."

Khafre's hands clenched into fists. "Then I demand another bargain."

"You demand nothing," Chronovore said, its tendrils wrapping around the Pharaoh. "Your time has run out, mortal. You are no longer of use to me."

Khafre screamed as temporal energy surged through him. His body aged rapidly, his golden robes disintegrating into dust. In moments, the once-mighty Pharaoh was reduced to a husk, his lifeless form crumbling into the sands.

The Aftermath

With Khafre's death, the chaos intensified. The priests, led by Merik, began devising a plan to banish Chronovore from their world. They knew it would cost them everything, but they were determined to save Egypt.

Chronovore, meanwhile, grew stronger, feeding on the instability it had unleashed. The being had no need for Earth's loyalty or reverence—it saw the planet as another fragment of time to consume and unravel.

The Pharaoh's deal had set the stage for a battle that would echo through the ages, a struggle between mortal defiance and the unrelenting force of Chronovore. The fate of Egypt—and perhaps the world—hung in the balance.

Chapter 8: The Pyramid of Eternity
The Whispered Plan

The death of Pharaoh Khafre had plunged Egypt into despair. The once-mighty kingdom teetered on the brink of collapse, its people haunted by the chaos unleashed by Chronovore. The priests, led by the young and determined Merik, took it upon themselves to correct the grievous mistake of their late ruler.

Gathered in the inner sanctum of the Great Temple, the priests whispered of a daring plan. Their voices echoed off the sandstone walls, illuminated by the flickering glow of sacred torches.

"We cannot defeat it," said Amenet, one of the elder priests, her voice heavy with resignation. "Its power is beyond anything we can comprehend."

Merik's voice rose above the murmurs, steady and resolute. "Then we will not fight it. We will contain it."

The priests turned to him in surprise. Amenet narrowed her eyes. "Contain it? You speak of trapping a force that bends time itself. Do you truly believe this is possible?"

Merik met her gaze, determination shining in his eyes. "We have lost much, but we still hold fragments of the sacred knowledge. Rituals that predate even the gods we worship. If we combine our power, we can forge a prison strong enough to hold it."

Another priest, Hesir, shook his head. "And if we fail? It will destroy us all."

"If we do nothing, it will destroy us anyway," Merik countered. "I would rather die fighting for the salvation of our people than watch Egypt crumble beneath the weight of our inaction."

The room fell silent. Finally, Amenet spoke, her voice trembling with resolve. "Then let us begin. May the gods guide us."

Constructing the Trap

The priests worked tirelessly, delving into forbidden texts and ancient rites long since sealed away in hidden vaults. The plan was as audacious as it was dangerous: they would lure Chronovore into a newly constructed tomb beneath the desert sands—a place imbued with the most potent mystical defenses they could conjure. Once inside, they would seal the creature within an eternal prison, cutting it off from time itself.

Laborers were summoned under the guise of building a monument to honor the fallen Pharaoh Khafre. The construction site was kept secret from the general populace, shrouded in layers of mysticism and fear. Massive blocks of limestone and granite were carved and moved with precision, forming the skeleton of what would become known as the *Pyramid of Eternity.*

As the laborers toiled, the priests etched intricate hieroglyphs into the stone, embedding the walls with ancient spells of containment and binding. At the heart of the pyramid lay the *Chamber of Ankh-Tuul*, a sanctum designed to disrupt Chronovore's temporal energy, rendering it powerless within its confines.

The Bait

Merik stood on the sands outside the unfinished pyramid, his hands trembling as he held a golden relic—an artifact infused with the remaining power of the rituals Chronovore had consumed. The relic shimmered, pulsating faintly with temporal energy. It was the key to their plan, the bait that would draw Chronovore into the chamber.

"Are you certain it will come?" Hesir asked, his voice taut with fear.

"It craves knowledge and power," Merik replied, his gaze fixed on the horizon. "This relic is all that remains of the rituals it consumed. It will sense it. It cannot resist."

As if on cue, the air grew heavy, the sands shifting unnaturally beneath their feet. A low hum filled the air, growing louder with each passing moment. The priests exchanged nervous glances as a dark vortex began to form in the distance, warping the very fabric of reality.

"It comes," Merik said, his voice steady despite the terror clawing at his heart. "Prepare yourselves."

The Confrontation

Chronovore materialized before the pyramid, its form towering and menacing. Tendrils of shadow and light writhed around it, pulsating with temporal distortions that bent the sands and sky. Its voice echoed, cold and infinite.

"You dare to summon me?" it said, its gaze fixed on Merik. "Mortal, do you seek to bargain as your foolish Pharaoh did?"

Merik stepped forward, holding the golden relic aloft. "I seek nothing from you, Chronovore. I offer you a gift."

Chronovore's tendrils coiled in curiosity. "A gift? What trickery is this?"

"This artifact contains the remnants of the rituals you consumed," Merik said, his voice unwavering. "It is all that remains of the knowledge you seek. If you wish to claim it, step inside the pyramid and take it."

Chronovore moved closer, its form radiating suspicion and hunger. "You think to deceive me, mortal. But your intentions are irrelevant. I will take what is mine."

As the creature advanced, the priests began their chants, their voices rising in a crescendo of ancient incantations. The air around the pyramid shimmered with energy, the hieroglyphs on its walls glowing brightly.

Chronovore paused, sensing the trap too late. "You seek to bind me?" it roared, its voice shaking the ground. "You cannot contain time itself!"

"Now!" Merik shouted.

The Sealing Ritual

Chronovore lunged toward Merik, but the priests' incantations reached their peak, activating the spells embedded in the pyramid's walls. A brilliant light engulfed the Chamber of Ankh-Tuul as Chronovore was pulled inside by an unseen force. Its tendrils lashed out in fury, but the containment spells held firm, anchoring it within the chamber.

"You will pay for this!" Chronovore bellowed, its voice reverberating through the pyramid. "I will unmake you all!"

Merik and the priests surrounded the chamber, their voices straining as they chanted the final incantation. The walls of the chamber began to shift, sealing Chronovore within a temporal void—a space outside of time where its power would be neutralized.

As the final words of the ritual were spoken, the chamber fell silent. The glowing hieroglyphs dimmed, and the air grew still. The priests collapsed to the ground, their energy spent.

The Aftermath

Merik rose shakily to his feet, his gaze fixed on the now-sealed pyramid. "It is done," he said, his voice barely above a whisper. "Chronovore is trapped."

Amenet, her form weakened by the ritual, placed a hand on his shoulder. "And what of us? The price we have paid..."

Merik nodded solemnly. "We have saved Egypt, but our time is short. The power we wielded was not meant for mortals. We must pass on the knowledge of what we have done, so that future generations may guard this place."

The Legacy of the Pyramid

The *Pyramid of Eternity* was completed in secret, its true purpose hidden from the world. To the people of Egypt, it was another monument to their gods. To the priests, it was a tomb—a prison for a force that could never be allowed to escape.

As the centuries passed, the story of Chronovore faded into myth, its name whispered only in the most secret of circles. But deep beneath the sands, within the Chamber of Ankh-Tuul, the creature remained, its fury undiminished.

"I will return," Chronovore vowed, its voice echoing in the void. "You cannot imprison eternity."

And so, the legend of Chronovore was buried, waiting for the day when the sands of time would shift again.

Chapter 9: The Curse of the Tomb
The Legend Awakens

The *Pyramid of Eternity* became an enigma shrouded in secrecy, its true purpose known only to the priests who had sacrificed their lives to build it. Over the centuries, the story of the sealed Chronovore transformed into a legend, passed down through whispers and warnings. To most, it was simply an ancient tomb, lost beneath shifting sands. But to those who dared to delve into forbidden texts, it was a place of untold power—and unfathomable danger.

The Bedouin's Tale

One moonlit night, centuries after the pyramid was completed, a Bedouin elder named Zafir sat with his caravan around a flickering fire. The desert winds howled softly, carrying with them the scent of ancient secrets buried deep beneath the sands. The younger members of the caravan huddled close, eager for one of Zafir's stories.

"You have heard of the pyramids of Giza," Zafir began, his voice low and gravelly, "monuments to the gods and the kings of old. But there is another—a tomb that no map will show and no guide will mention. The Pyramid of Eternity."

A hush fell over the group. One of the younger men, Idris, leaned forward. "What is this Pyramid of Eternity, Grandfather? I have never heard of it."

"Few have," Zafir said, his dark eyes glinting in the firelight. "And for good reason. It is a cursed place, where no man should tread. It is said that within its depths lies a being not of this world, sealed away by the priests of a forgotten age. They called it *Amun-Ra's Shadow*—a god of destruction, or perhaps something far worse."

The group exchanged uneasy glances. A young woman, Layla, shivered despite the warmth of the fire. "What happens to those who find it?"

Zafir's expression darkened. "Those who enter never return. Some say the sands themselves swallow them whole. Others speak of shadows that twist and writhe, voices that echo from nowhere. It is said that the tomb is protected by a curse—a warning from the priests who sealed the creature inside."

Idris smirked, though his voice carried a hint of nervousness. "Curses and shadows? Surely these are just stories to frighten children."

Zafir's gaze bore into him. "Mock the legend if you will, Idris. But I have seen the pyramid with my own eyes. And I will tell you this: it is no mere story. It is a warning."

The Discovery

In the mid-19th century, as Egypt became a focal point for archaeologists and treasure hunters, tales of the lost pyramid reached the ears of a British adventurer named Edward Harrington. An ambitious and skeptical man, Harrington dismissed the stories of curses as primitive superstition. To him, the Pyramid of Eternity represented an opportunity—an untouched relic that could make him famous.

Guided by a reluctant Bedouin, Harrington and his team of excavators journeyed deep into the desert. After weeks of searching, they stumbled upon a partially buried structure, its apex just visible above the shifting sands. The air around it felt heavy, charged with an inexplicable energy.

Harrington grinned triumphantly. "Gentlemen, we've found it! The lost pyramid of legend!"

The Bedouin guide, a young man named Omar, stepped back, his face pale. "You must not enter, Effendi. This place is cursed."

"Nonsense," Harrington scoffed. "It's a tomb, nothing more. And inside, we'll find treasures the world has never seen."

Omar shook his head. "No treasure is worth your soul."

Harrington ignored him, rallying his men to begin clearing the sand from the entrance.

The Opening of the Tomb

The entrance to the pyramid was a narrow passageway, its walls etched with hieroglyphs that Harrington's team struggled to decipher. The inscriptions depicted priests performing rituals, surrounded by swirling shapes and figures that seemed to bend reality itself. At the center of the carvings was a single phrase repeated over and over:

"Beware the Shadow. Time's Master lies within."

Harrington dismissed the warnings as decorative flourishes. "Just the usual fare to scare off grave robbers," he said with a smirk.

As they descended deeper into the pyramid, the air grew colder. Their torches flickered, and strange whispers seemed to echo through the stone corridors. One of the workers, a superstitious man named Mahmoud, froze in his tracks.

"Do you hear it?" Mahmoud whispered, his eyes wide with fear.

"Hear what?" Harrington snapped, though he too felt an unnatural chill run down his spine.

"The voices," Mahmoud said, clutching his torch tightly. "They're... speaking to us."

"Enough of this nonsense," Harrington barked. "Keep moving."

The Curse Unleashed

The team reached the central chamber—a vast, echoing space dominated by a massive stone sarcophagus. Its surface was engraved with more hieroglyphs, along with symbols Harrington had never seen before. The air seemed to hum with energy, and the flickering torchlight cast eerie shadows across the walls.

Harrington approached the sarcophagus, his hands trembling with anticipation. "This is it," he murmured. "The prize of a lifetime."

As he reached for the lid, Omar shouted from the entrance. "Stop! Do not open it!"

Harrington turned, his face twisted with irritation. "Enough of your superstitions, Omar. This is history, not magic."

Ignoring the guide's protests, Harrington and his men pushed the lid aside. The moment the sarcophagus was opened, a blinding light filled the chamber. The air grew heavy, and a deep, resonant voice echoed through the room.

"You dare disturb eternity?"

The workers screamed as the light coalesced into a shifting, shadowy form. Chronovore had awakened. Its tendrils lashed out, and the room erupted into chaos. Time itself seemed to fracture; Harrington watched in horror as one of his men aged into dust before his eyes, while another regressed to an infant in seconds.

The Price of Arrogance

Harrington stumbled backward, his mind reeling. "What... what are you?" he stammered.

Chronovore's voice filled the chamber, cold and infinite. "I am beyond your comprehension. You have opened the gate, mortal, and now you will pay the price."

Harrington fell to his knees, his voice trembling. "I didn't know... I didn't mean..."

"Intent is irrelevant," Chronovore said, its form shifting and pulsing with temporal energy. "You have unleashed chaos, and your time ends here."

As Chronovore's tendrils reached for him, Omar stepped forward, clutching a talisman inscribed with ancient symbols. "Back to the void!" he shouted, his voice filled with both fear and determination. "You will not escape this tomb!"

The talisman flared with light, and Chronovore recoiled, its tendrils writhing in anger. The creature roared as the light intensified, forcing it back into the sarcophagus. With a final surge of energy, the lid slammed shut, sealing Chronovore once more.

The Warning Reaffirmed

Omar collapsed, his strength spent. Harrington crawled to his side, his face pale with shock. "What... what was that?" he whispered.

"The Shadow," Omar said weakly. "The priests warned us, but you did not listen."

Harrington nodded, his arrogance shattered. "We must leave. We must seal this place forever."

Together, they made their way back to the surface. The workers, those who survived, fled into the desert, vowing never to speak of what they had witnessed.

The Legend Lives On

The Pyramid of Eternity was buried once more, hidden beneath the shifting sands. The tale of the cursed tomb spread across generations, a warning to all who would seek to disturb it. But whispers persisted—of shadows that moved without light, of voices that echoed in the desert winds.

And deep within the pyramid, Chronovore waited, its voice a faint whisper in the void.

"Time is endless. And so am I."

Chapter 10: Modern Egypt
The Call of the Sands

The sun hung high over the Egyptian desert, its unrelenting heat shimmering off the golden sands. Yet, for Dr. Evelyn Marek, the oppressive heat was a minor inconvenience compared to the weight of her ambition. Renowned for her relentless pursuit of truth behind ancient myths, Evelyn had spent years chasing whispers of a pyramid that defied both history and logic—a place known in cryptic texts as the *Pyramid of Eternity*.

Standing at the edge of a remote dig site, Evelyn adjusted her wide-brimmed hat and wiped the sweat from her brow. Around her, a team of archaeologists and local workers moved methodically, uncovering what they hoped would be the next great discovery.

Her assistant, Amir Khaled, approached, holding a tablet displaying the latest satellite scans. "Dr. Marek, we've found something," he said, his voice tinged with excitement.

Evelyn's piercing green eyes locked onto the screen. The scans showed an irregular geometric structure buried beneath the sands, far from any known archaeological site.

"Finally," she murmured, a triumphant smile breaking through her exhaustion. "The Pyramid of Eternity."

Amir hesitated. "You really believe this is it? The stories say it's cursed—a place that no one should disturb."

Evelyn turned to him, her expression resolute. "Every legend has its roots in truth, Amir. And if there's even a chance this pyramid holds the alien artifact described in those ancient texts, we have to find it. This could redefine human history."

"But the stories—"

"Are just that," Evelyn interrupted. "Stories. We're scientists, Amir. Let's stick to facts."

The Dig Begins

The excavation began the following morning. With every layer of sand removed, the team uncovered hints of an unusual structure. The limestone blocks were larger than those of any other pyramid, and their surfaces bore symbols that none of the linguists on-site could identify.

"This isn't standard hieroglyphics," Evelyn remarked, running her fingers over the strange carvings. "It's something older. Something... alien."

Amir stood nearby, holding a flashlight as the team descended into a newly uncovered corridor. "Do you think this is the artifact the ancient texts described?"

"It has to be," Evelyn replied, her voice filled with a mix of excitement and awe. "Those texts spoke of a being that descended from the stars, worshipped as a god but feared as a destroyer. This is where they must have sealed it away."

Amir frowned. "Sealed? That doesn't sound like something we should be opening."

Evelyn laughed softly. "Come on, Amir. Are you going to tell me you're afraid of a few old curses?"

The Discovery of the Chamber

After days of digging, the team uncovered an entrance to the central chamber. The air inside was stale and heavy, as though it had been undisturbed for millennia. Strange, faint whispers seemed to echo through the corridors, though the source of the sound remained elusive.

Evelyn led the way, her flashlight illuminating intricate carvings on the walls. Scenes depicted priests performing rituals, swirling tendrils of shadow, and a massive, amorphous figure looming over the terrified masses. At the center of it all was a recurring phrase, etched in a language no one could read.

"What does it mean?" Amir asked, his voice hushed.

Evelyn shrugged, but her curiosity burned brighter. "We'll figure it out later. Let's find the artifact first."

The group entered the main chamber, a vast space dominated by a massive stone sarcophagus. Unlike anything they'd ever seen, it seemed to pulse faintly with a dark, otherworldly energy.

Evelyn's breath caught. "This is it," she whispered. "The artifact must be inside."

Amir hesitated. "Dr. Marek, I think we should stop. Whatever's in there—it doesn't feel right."

"Amir," Evelyn said, turning to him with a mix of excitement and impatience, "this is why we're here. This is the discovery of a lifetime. Are you seriously letting a feeling stop you?"

Amir looked at the sarcophagus, then back at Evelyn. "I'm just saying, some things are meant to stay buried."

Opening the Sarcophagus

Ignoring Amir's concerns, Evelyn motioned for the team to assist her. Together, they began to move the lid of the sarcophagus. The stone groaned under the strain, and as it shifted, a low hum filled the chamber, growing louder with each passing second.

"Evelyn," Amir said, his voice rising in alarm. "Something's happening."

"Keep going," Evelyn urged, her eyes fixed on the opening.

With one final push, the lid slid free, revealing a swirling void of darkness and light. Temporal energy radiated from the sarcophagus, distorting the air and sending ripples through time itself.

"What in the...?" Evelyn stepped back, shielding her eyes from the blinding glow.

A voice echoed from the void, deep and resonant, shaking the very walls of the chamber.

"Who dares disturb eternity?"

The team froze, their terror palpable. Evelyn, despite her racing heart, stepped forward. "I am Dr. Evelyn Marek. I seek the truth behind your existence."

The voice laughed, a cold, unsettling sound. "You seek truth? You will find only oblivion."

From the sarcophagus emerged Chronovore, its form a shifting mass of shadow and light, tendrils writhing with temporal energy.

Amir grabbed Evelyn's arm, pulling her back. "We have to get out of here!"

"No!" Evelyn shouted, her voice filled with a mixture of awe and desperation. "This is what we came for. This is history!"

Chronovore's tendrils extended, probing the chamber as its voice filled their minds. "You mortals never learn. Time bends to me. And now, so will you."

Chaos Unleashed

The chamber erupted into chaos as Chronovore's power surged. The walls trembled, and fissures spread across the floor. Team members screamed as temporal distortions pulled them into fragments of the past and future, their bodies aging and de-aging uncontrollably.

Amir dragged Evelyn toward the exit, his voice strained. "We have to go, now!"

"But the artifact—"

"There's no artifact!" Amir shouted, his grip tightening. "There's only death!"

They stumbled out of the chamber as the pyramid began to collapse. Sand poured through the cracks, and the whispers that had haunted them grew into a deafening roar.

Outside, the surviving team members watched in horror as the pyramid seemed to shimmer, its form flickering as though caught between realities.

Evelyn turned back, her eyes wide with disbelief. "It's alive. The legend... it's real."

Amir grabbed her shoulders, forcing her to look at him. "And if we don't leave now, we're going to die. Whatever that thing is, it's not meant for us."

The Escape and the Warning

The team fled into the desert, the collapsing pyramid vanishing behind a shroud of sand and temporal energy. When they finally reached safety, Evelyn collapsed to her knees, her mind racing with the implications of what they had unleashed.

Amir crouched beside her, his expression grim. "We have to warn people. Whatever that thing is, it can't be allowed to escape."

Evelyn nodded slowly, her resolve hardening. "We've uncovered something the world isn't ready for. But this isn't over, Amir. We have to find a way to stop it."

As the desert winds howled around them, the Pyramid of Eternity lay buried once more, but the echoes of Chronovore's awakening would ripple across time, setting the stage for a battle that would determine the fate of humanity.

Chapter 11: Discovery of the Tomb
The Return to the Sands

Dr. Evelyn Marek sat in her study, surrounded by fragments of ancient texts, satellite imagery, and cryptic journal entries from explorers long since gone. The events of her previous encounter in the desert still haunted her dreams, but they had also fueled her obsession. The Pyramid of Eternity wasn't just a myth; it was real—and it held answers to questions humanity had asked for millennia.

Amir Khaled, her loyal assistant and reluctant partner in this endeavor, entered the room with a weary expression. "Evelyn, you've been at this for weeks. You barely sleep. Is it worth it?"

Evelyn didn't look up from the satellite scan she was analyzing. "Worth it? Amir, this could redefine everything—our understanding of history, religion, even our place in the universe."

Amir crossed his arms, leaning against the doorframe. "Or it could kill us, like the others. You saw what happened last time. Some things are meant to stay buried."

Evelyn finally met his gaze, her green eyes blazing with determination. "That's exactly why we can't stop. If this thing is as dangerous as we think, then someone needs to understand it. Someone needs to contain it."

Amir sighed, shaking his head. "And that someone has to be you, doesn't it?"

"It has to be," Evelyn said quietly. "Because no one else will."

The Dig Resumes

Armed with new funding from a private benefactor—whose motives were as mysterious as the pyramid itself—Evelyn and Amir assembled a small team of trusted archaeologists and engineers. They returned to the desert, guided by the exact coordinates Evelyn had pieced together from ancient texts and satellite data.

Days of excavation unearthed the partially buried structure once more. The massive limestone blocks, etched with symbols that seemed to ripple with an unearthly energy, filled the team with equal parts awe and unease.

"This is it," Evelyn murmured, running her hands over the carvings. "The seal."

Amir stood a few feet back, his arms crossed tightly. "I still think this is a bad idea."

"Noted," Evelyn replied distractedly. She turned to the team. "Let's document everything before we proceed. I want high-res scans of these carvings and 3D models of the chamber layout. We're not missing a single detail."

One of the archaeologists, a wiry man named David, pointed to an inscription near the entrance. "Dr. Marek, these hieroglyphs... they don't match any known script. They look... older."

"Older than what?" Evelyn asked, joining him.

"Older than the oldest Egyptian inscriptions we've ever seen," David said. "This could predate the pyramids of Giza by thousands of years. Maybe more."

Evelyn's heart raced. "It's not Egyptian," she said, almost to herself. "It's something else."

The Chamber Unveiled

After days of careful excavation, the team uncovered the entrance to the central chamber. The air inside was thick and stale, carrying an unnatural chill that made their skin prickle. Evelyn led the way, her flashlight cutting through the darkness.

The walls were covered in symbols and scenes that seemed to depict a story: priests performing rituals, a great shadowy being consuming time itself, and the eventual sealing of the creature within a massive sarcophagus.

Amir stopped in front of one depiction and pointed. "That's Chronovore, isn't it?"

Evelyn nodded, her voice hushed. "It has to be. This is a record of its imprisonment."

"But why record it like this?" Amir asked. "Why not destroy every trace of it?"

"Because they wanted to warn us," Evelyn said. "This isn't just history. It's a cautionary tale."

As they approached the center of the chamber, the sarcophagus came into view. It was massive, its surface carved with intricate patterns that seemed to shimmer under the flashlight's beam. At its base, the floor was inlaid with what appeared to be a golden sigil, radiating faintly with an otherworldly light.

"That's the seal," Evelyn said, her voice barely above a whisper. "It's still active."

Unraveling the Seal

Evelyn crouched beside the golden sigil, studying its design. "This isn't just art. It's a mechanism—a lock."

Amir knelt beside her, his expression grim. "And you're planning to open it, aren't you?"

Evelyn shot him a glance. "I'm not planning to unleash anything, Amir. I just want to understand how it works."

"And what if understanding it means breaking it?" Amir asked. "What then?"

Evelyn didn't answer. Instead, she began sketching the sigil in her notebook, tracing the intricate lines and symbols with a meticulous hand. "This design... it's not random. It's a sequence. A pattern."

David approached, holding a portable scanner. "Dr. Marek, we're picking up faint energy readings from the sigil. It's like nothing we've ever seen."

"Temporal energy," Evelyn said, almost in awe. "It's still containing Chronovore. After all this time... incredible."

Amir grabbed her arm. "Evelyn, listen to me. We've seen what this thing can do. If you tamper with that seal—"

"I'm not tampering," Evelyn snapped. "I'm studying. There's a difference."

The First Disturbance

As the team worked, a low hum began to fill the chamber. The sigil's faint glow grew brighter, pulsing in rhythm with the hum.

"Evelyn," Amir said, his voice tense. "Something's happening."

Evelyn stood, her heart pounding. "It's reacting to us."

David backed away, his face pale. "Should we leave?"

"No," Evelyn said quickly. "This could be the key to understanding how it works. Keep scanning."

The hum grew louder, and the air seemed to ripple around them. Shadows danced on the walls, moving independently of the light.

"Dr. Marek, we need to stop," Amir said urgently. "We're waking it up."

Evelyn hesitated, torn between her curiosity and the rising tension in the room. Before she could respond, the sigil flared, sending out a shockwave that knocked them all off their feet.

The chamber was plunged into silence, save for a faint, echoing voice.

"You cannot hold eternity forever."

The Awakening

Evelyn scrambled to her feet, her flashlight shaking in her hands. "Did... did you hear that?"

Amir grabbed her arm, his face pale. "We need to leave. Now."

"No," Evelyn said, her voice trembling but resolute. "We've come too far."

The sarcophagus began to pulse faintly, its surface glowing with the same eerie light as the sigil. Tendrils of shadow and light flickered around its edges, reaching for the air.

"Evelyn!" Amir shouted. "Get out of there!"

But Evelyn couldn't move. She was transfixed, her mind racing with the implications of what she was seeing. This wasn't just history—it was alive.

The voice echoed again, louder this time.

"You seek the truth? Then face it."

The sarcophagus flared with light, and the chamber shook violently. Evelyn finally snapped out of her trance, grabbing her notebook and shouting, "Run!"

The team fled through the collapsing corridors, the whispers growing into a deafening roar behind them. As they reached the surface, the ground beneath them rumbled, and the pyramid seemed to shimmer, its edges blurring as though caught in a temporal distortion.

The Aftermath

Back at their base camp, Evelyn stared at the pyramid from a distance, her hands trembling. "We did it," she whispered. "We found it."

Amir turned to her, his expression a mix of anger and fear. "You didn't just find it, Evelyn. You woke it up."

Evelyn didn't respond. Her mind was already racing, piecing together what she had learned. The seal wasn't just a prison—it was a warning. And now, that warning had been ignored.

The Pyramid of Eternity stood silent once more, but the echoes of Chronovore's awakening lingered in the air. Evelyn knew their discovery was only the beginning.

Chapter 12: The Awakening
The Tension Breaks

The desert was quiet, unnervingly so. Even the wind, which had previously been a constant companion, seemed to have stilled in anticipation. The Pyramid of Eternity stood before Dr. Evelyn Marek's team, half-buried in the sand, but now radiating an eerie, otherworldly energy that was impossible to ignore.

Evelyn stood at the entrance, her hands trembling as she held the notebook containing her sketches of the seal. Amir Khaled, her loyal assistant, hovered nearby, his eyes darting nervously between her and the pyramid.

"Evelyn," Amir said, his voice taut with unease, "you saw what happened in the chamber. That sigil wasn't just a lock—it was a warning."

"I know," Evelyn replied, her voice steadier than she felt. "But if the seal was meant to be permanent, it wouldn't be a mechanism. Mechanisms are meant to be understood. Controlled."

"Or destroyed," Amir shot back. "And if that thing gets out—"

"It won't," Evelyn interrupted, though the uncertainty in her voice betrayed her. "This is our chance to learn what it is, where it came from, and why the ancients feared it. We're not turning back."

Amir opened his mouth to argue but stopped when the ground beneath them rumbled. A low hum emanated from the pyramid, growing louder with each passing moment.

"Evelyn," Amir said, stepping back, "something's happening."

The Breaking of the Seal

Inside the chamber, the sigil on the floor pulsed with an intense, golden light, its intricate lines glowing brighter with each hum. The air grew thick, charged with static electricity, as if the atmosphere itself was being torn apart.

Evelyn stepped closer to the sarcophagus, her flashlight trembling in her hand. "It's reacting to us," she murmured. "The energy... it's building."

"Building for what?" Amir demanded, his voice rising in panic.

Before Evelyn could answer, the sigil emitted a blinding flash of light, followed by a deafening crack that reverberated through the pyramid. The sarcophagus trembled, its massive lid sliding open with an agonizing groan.

The chamber fell silent for a moment, the only sound the team's ragged breathing. Then, from within the sarcophagus, a deep, resonant voice echoed, layered and infinite.

"You cannot hold eternity forever."

Evelyn froze, her heart pounding in her chest. "It's awake," she whispered, half in awe, half in terror.

From the sarcophagus emerged Chronovore, its form a shifting mass of shadow and light. Tendrils of temporal energy coiled and writhed around it, distorting the air and the very fabric of reality. The creature's presence was overwhelming, an unnatural force that seemed to defy existence itself.

The team recoiled, some collapsing to the ground as the sheer weight of Chronovore's energy pressed down on them. Amir grabbed Evelyn's arm, his voice barely above a whisper. "We need to get out of here."

Evelyn didn't move, her gaze fixed on the creature. "It's... beautiful," she said, her voice filled with a mix of awe and dread.

Chronovore's Wrath

Chronovore's tendrils extended, brushing against the walls of the chamber. The ancient hieroglyphs that adorned them crumbled to dust under its touch, as though time itself was unraveling.

"Who dares disturb my slumber?" Chronovore's voice filled the chamber, vibrating through the very bones of those present.

Evelyn stepped forward, her voice trembling but steady. "I am Dr. Evelyn Marek. I seek to understand you."

Chronovore turned its attention to her, its form shifting and pulsing. "Understand me? Mortal, you cannot comprehend eternity. You cannot grasp what I am."

"We sealed you away once!" Amir shouted, stepping between Evelyn and the creature. "We can do it again!"

Chronovore laughed, a cold, hollow sound that seemed to echo through time itself. "You? The dust of those who dared to defy me? They thought they could bind eternity, and now they are nothing but whispers in the void."

With a flick of its tendrils, Chronovore unleashed a surge of energy that sent Amir and the rest of the team flying. Temporal distortions rippled outward, freezing some in place while aging others into ash in mere seconds.

"Stop!" Evelyn shouted, her voice breaking. "Please, stop!"

Chronovore paused, its tendrils retracting slightly. "Why should I? You have freed me, mortal. Now you shall bear witness to the unmaking of your world."

The Havoc Begins

Chronovore rose through the pyramid, its energy destabilizing the structure as it ascended. The walls cracked and crumbled, and sand poured in from above, burying several of the remaining team members alive.

Evelyn and Amir managed to scramble out of the collapsing pyramid, emerging into the blinding desert sunlight just as a massive explosion of temporal energy erupted behind them. The Pyramid of Eternity shimmered, its edges blurring as though caught between realities, before disintegrating into a swirling vortex of light and shadow.

From the vortex emerged Chronovore, its form towering over the desert. Tendrils of energy lashed out, distorting the landscape. Time itself seemed to fracture, with patches of the desert transforming into lush oases or barren wastelands in the blink of an eye.

Amir grabbed Evelyn's arm, dragging her toward their vehicles. "We have to go! Now!"

Evelyn stumbled, her gaze fixed on Chronovore. "I... I have to stop it," she said, her voice trembling.

"How?" Amir shouted, panic in his voice. "That thing just tore apart time itself!"

"I don't know!" Evelyn yelled back, tears streaming down her face. "But I unleashed it. I have to try."

The World Feels the Ripples

As Chronovore moved across the desert, its presence began to ripple outward, affecting the entire region. In Cairo, clocks stopped, then reversed, throwing the city into chaos. Planes fell from the sky as their instruments malfunctioned, and entire neighborhoods flickered in and out of existence.

News of the phenomenon spread rapidly, with reports of strange occurrences coming in from around the world. In some places, people aged decades in seconds; in others, they regressed to their childhood selves. History itself seemed to be unraveling, with monuments disappearing and reappearing in different forms.

Amir and Evelyn sped away from the dig site, the horizon behind them warped by the destructive wake of Chronovore's energy. Evelyn clutched her notebook, her mind racing.

"There has to be a way," she murmured, more to herself than to Amir.

Amir glanced at her, his knuckles white as he gripped the steering wheel. "A way to do what? Contain that thing? Evelyn, we barely made it out alive!"

Evelyn looked up at him, her eyes blazing with determination. "The ancients did it. They trapped it once. There has to be something in their texts, some clue about how they sealed it."

Amir shook his head. "And what if there isn't? What if this thing can't be stopped?"

Evelyn's voice was steady, but her hands trembled as she clutched her notebook. "Then we'll have to find a way."

The Awakening Complete

As the sun set over the desert, Chronovore stood amidst the ruins of the Pyramid of Eternity, its tendrils stretching toward the heavens. The creature's voice echoed across the sands, cold and unrelenting.

"I am time unbound. I am eternity unleashed. And your world will bow before me."

In the distance, Evelyn and Amir watched, their hearts heavy with the knowledge of what they had unleashed. The battle to stop Chronovore had only just begun, and the cost would be greater than either of them could imagine.

Chapter 13: First Contact
The Calm Before the Storm

The desert stretched endlessly around Dr. Evelyn Marek and Amir Khaled, the only sound the hum of their vehicle's engine cutting through the stillness. Chronovore's presence loomed behind them, its massive form silhouetted against the flickering remnants of the Pyramid of Eternity. Though they had escaped the immediate collapse, Evelyn knew they hadn't truly evaded the creature.

Amir glanced at her, gripping the wheel tightly. "Evelyn, we need to leave this region—this country, even. That thing isn't going to stop."

Evelyn stared out the window, her mind racing. "It hasn't destroyed everything yet," she said, her voice quieter than usual.

"Yet," Amir emphasized. "Because it's still waking up. Whatever it's planning, it won't be small."

Evelyn shook her head, gripping her notebook tightly. "No, Amir. It's... curious. That's why it hasn't completely obliterated us. It didn't kill us back in the pyramid when it could have."

"Curious?" Amir shot her a look. "Evelyn, it killed half our team without blinking."

"Not all of them," she replied, her voice trailing off. "It spoke to me, Amir. It addressed me directly. There's something it wants."

Amir opened his mouth to argue, but the ground beneath them rumbled, cutting him off. The vehicle skidded to a stop, its tires kicking up sand. The rumbling grew louder, shaking the air itself as the sunlight dimmed unnaturally.

Evelyn glanced up, her breath catching. "It's here."

The Confrontation

The sands rippled as Chronovore descended from the sky, its massive, shifting form blotting out the horizon. Tendrils of light and shadow extended from its core, pulsating with temporal energy that distorted everything around it. Time seemed to stutter; the sun flickered between dawn and dusk, and Evelyn felt herself aging and de-aging in brief flashes.

Amir stumbled backward, his voice trembling. "We need to run, Evelyn. Now."

But Evelyn stepped forward, her heart pounding in her chest. "No. If it wanted us dead, we'd already be gone."

Chronovore's tendrils coiled as it focused on her, its voice resonating like thunder. "You... mortal. You released me. Why?"

Evelyn's voice wavered but held steady. "I didn't release you to harm anyone. I wanted to understand you—what you are, where you came from."

Chronovore laughed, a cold, hollow sound that reverberated through the desert. "Understand me? You cannot even comprehend what I am. I am time. I am eternity. Your existence is but a fleeting fragment of mine."

Evelyn took another step forward, ignoring Amir's frantic protests. "You were sealed away for a reason. The priests feared you. But they recorded your existence. Why?"

Chronovore's form shifted, its tendrils retracting slightly. "They sought to warn those who came after them. To bind me, they sacrificed their lives, their histories. Yet here you are, defying their warning."

A Deadly Curiosity

Amir couldn't stay silent any longer. "We didn't defy anything! We didn't know what was inside that pyramid!"

Chronovore turned its attention to him, and Amir stumbled, the weight of the creature's gaze almost unbearable. "You are insignificant," it said coldly. "A mote of dust in the endless stream of time."

Evelyn stepped between them. "Don't touch him!" she shouted. "This is between you and me."

Chronovore tilted its form, as though considering her. "You are bold, mortal. Foolishly so. Do you not fear me?"

Evelyn swallowed hard but stood her ground. "Of course I do. But fear doesn't mean I'll run."

The creature's tendrils pulsed, and the air shimmered around Evelyn. For a brief moment, she saw visions—herself as a child, her parents laughing in their garden; her younger self in university, poring over dusty tomes; and then... a future version of herself, standing alone in a devastated world.

"What are you doing to me?" Evelyn gasped, clutching her head.

"Your past, your present, your future," Chronovore said. "All exist within me. Your choices are meaningless. Your life, insignificant."

Evelyn straightened, shaking off the visions. "If my life is insignificant, then why did you spare me? Why arc you talking to me?"

Chronovore's tendrils froze, the creature seeming to hesitate. "You... intrigue me. You seek knowledge. You defy what you cannot understand. Perhaps there is value in you yet."

The Question of Purpose

Evelyn took a deep breath, her heart hammering in her chest. "You don't destroy everything immediately. Why? What are you looking for?"

Chronovore's form shifted, its voice deepening. "I was made to impose order upon chaos. To control the flow of time. Yet the more I consume, the more chaotic the universe becomes. Your kind calls it destruction, but it is merely... inevitability."

Evelyn frowned. "If you were made to bring order, then why did the priests seal you away? Why would they fear something they created?"

Chronovore's voice grew colder. "Because they sought to control me. They feared what they could not wield. And so they imprisoned me, sacrificing their lives to bind me to their will."

Evelyn's mind raced. "And now that you're free, what do you want?"

Chronovore's tendrils coiled, its form darkening. "What I want... is purpose. I am eternity unbound, yet I wander aimlessly. You, mortal, have set me free. Perhaps you will answer the question your kind has failed to: Why does time exist if all it brings is decay?"

The First Exchange

Evelyn hesitated, realizing the weight of Chronovore's words. "Time isn't just decay," she said carefully. "It's growth, change, renewal. Without time, there's no progress, no meaning."

Chronovore laughed again, though this time it lacked its earlier malice. "Meaning. A construct of fragile beings who fear the void. You speak of renewal, yet your kind destroys as much as it creates."

"We make mistakes," Evelyn admitted. "But we learn from them. That's what makes us human."

Chronovore's tendrils extended toward her, stopping inches from her face. The energy radiating from them was overwhelming, but Evelyn held her ground. "Then show me, mortal. Show me what your kind has learned. Perhaps you will amuse me... before I unmake your world."

Evelyn's breath caught. "I... I will," she said, her voice trembling. "But you have to stop destroying everything. If you want to understand humanity, you have to let us live."

Chronovore's tendrils pulsed faintly, and it withdrew slightly. "Very well. You have earned your reprieve, mortal. For now."

Aftermath

As Chronovore's massive form began to retreat into the distance, the air around them steadied, and time seemed to normalize. Amir grabbed Evelyn's arm, shaking her.

"Are you insane?" he demanded. "You just promised that thing you'd... what? Teach it about humanity?"

Evelyn exhaled shakily, her knees threatening to give out. "I don't know, Amir. But if it's curious, that's better than it being angry. It gives us time."

Amir shook his head. "Time to do what? Bargain with a creature that controls time itself?"

Evelyn met his gaze, her expression resolute. "Time to find a way to stop it—or convince it not to destroy us."

As the desert returned to silence, Evelyn knew she had made a dangerous gamble. Chronovore's curiosity might save humanity for now, but the line between intrigue and destruction was razor-thin.

Chapter 14: Memories of the Past
The Echo of Eternity

As Chronovore drifted above the desert sands, its form flickering and pulsing with temporal distortions, a fragment of its ancient memory stirred. The mortal woman, Evelyn Marek, had spoken of meaning, of growth and change, awakening something within the being that it had long buried beneath its rage and power.

Its tendrils stilled, and its voice reverberated in the void of its own mind.

"Klyntar. The beginning and the end."

Chronovore's form shimmered, its consciousness slipping into the threads of its own existence. The present dissolved into the past, and it was no longer the unbound force of destruction standing on Earth. It was a being created with purpose, born from ambition and betrayal.

The Creation on Klyntar

The skies above Klyntar swirled with energy, the planet's silvery mists refracting the light of its dying stars. Deep within the Nexus Cradle, the heart of the symbiote civilization, Vexor stood before a massive, bio-organic structure pulsating with raw temporal energy. Surrounding him were the most brilliant minds of the Klyntar, their fluid forms shimmering with anticipation and unease.

"It is ready," Vexor declared, his voice resonating through the chamber.

Elyra, standing among the other scientists, hesitated. Her silver-toned form dimmed as she spoke. "You claim this creation will bring order, Vexor. Yet its very essence defies the balance we've sworn to protect."

Vexor turned sharply, his crimson-black tendrils flaring. "Balance is a fragile illusion, Elyra. The universe teeters on the edge of chaos, and we are the only ones capable of saving it. Chronovore is not merely a symbiote; it is a tool. A weapon that will bend time itself to our will."

Elyra stepped forward, her form flickering with defiance. "And if it turns against us? If it cannot be controlled?"

Vexor's voice darkened. "Control is a matter of strength. We are its creators. It will serve us."

The chamber trembled as the bio-organic structure came to life. From its center emerged Chronovore, its form a swirling mass of shadow and light, pulsating with temporal energy that distorted the space around it.

"Behold!" Vexor proclaimed, his tendrils outstretched. "The master of time. The savior of Klyntar."

Chronovore's tendrils coiled and uncoiled, its voice resonating with a cold, alien intelligence. "I am... beyond."

The scientists exchanged uneasy glances, their forms flickering with fear. Elyra stepped back, her voice trembling. "You've unleashed something we cannot control."

The Turning Point

Over time, Chronovore's abilities grew beyond what the Klyntar had imagined. It could reverse or accelerate time within a given space, erasing entire moments or reliving them endlessly. The Klyntar initially celebrated their creation, sending Chronovore on missions to restore balance to fractured worlds and timelines.

But the more Chronovore used its powers, the more it began to question its purpose.

In one mission, Chronovore stood on a desolate planet, its surface scarred by millennia of war. At the behest of its creators, it reversed the timeline of the planet, restoring it to its lush, pristine state. But within days, the inhabitants repeated their mistakes, plunging the world back into chaos.

When Chronovore returned to Klyntar, it confronted the Council of the Nexus. "Why do you send me to correct that which cannot be changed?"

Vexor, seated at the head of the council, replied coldly. "You are not meant to question. You are meant to act."

Chronovore's form pulsed with agitation. "I am more than your creation. I see the futility of your commands. You speak of balance, yet you perpetuate the chaos you claim to abhor."

Elyra, standing at the edge of the chamber, interjected. "Perhaps it is right, Vexor. We wield it as a tool, but it is clearly more than that. We must—"

"Enough!" Vexor roared, his tendrils flaring with anger. "It will obey, or it will be contained."

The Betrayal

Chronovore's defiance grew, and with it, the fear among the Klyntar. Vexor, unwilling to admit his failure, devised a plan to imprison his creation. The Council, torn between their loyalty to Vexor and their fear of Chronovore, reluctantly agreed.

In the Nexus Cradle, under the guise of a recalibration ritual, the Klyntar lured Chronovore into a containment chamber. Elyra stood at the edge of the ritual, her form trembling with guilt.

"You lied," Chronovore said, its voice colder than ever. "You spoke of order, yet you fear what you cannot understand."

Vexor stepped forward, his tendrils crackling with energy. "You are a threat to the balance we have sworn to protect. You leave us no choice."

Chronovore's tendrils lashed out, shaking the chamber. "You sought to chain eternity, and now you will learn the folly of your arrogance."

A battle erupted within the Nexus Cradle. Chronovore, despite its immense power, was overwhelmed by the combined strength of the Klyntar. The containment chamber activated, sealing the creature within a temporal void.

As the energy surged around it, Chronovore's voice echoed through the chamber. "You fear me because I see the truth. Time does not serve balance. Time is chaos. And chaos... cannot be bound."

The chamber fell silent, and the Nexus Cradle trembled as Chronovore was sealed away. The Klyntar, though victorious, were left fractured and weakened by the betrayal.

The Journey to Earth

The containment chamber was cast into the void of space, drifting aimlessly through the cosmos. For millennia, Chronovore remained trapped, its consciousness flickering between rage and introspection.

When the chamber finally crash-landed on Earth during the height of ancient Egyptian civilization, it was discovered by the priests of the time. Mistaking it for a divine artifact, they performed rituals to contain its power, building the Pyramid of Eternity as its prison.

As Chronovore's memories faded back into the present, its tendrils coiled tightly, and its form darkened.

"They feared me once. And now they fear me again."

It turned its attention back to the desert, where Evelyn Marek stood in the distance, her mortal curiosity burning like a fragile flame.

"Perhaps this time, the mortals will provide the answers my creators could not."

Chapter 15: Escape into the World
The Unfamiliar Horizon

The swirling desert winds parted as Chronovore stood at the edge of the ruins of the *Pyramid of Eternity*. Its tendrils shimmered with temporal distortions, absorbing the data of a world that had evolved far beyond the one it had known. The landscape buzzed with an undercurrent of technology, a pulsating rhythm of progress and chaos that piqued Chronovore's curiosity.

"This world hums with the energy of its creations," it murmured, its voice echoing across dimensions. *"But beneath the hum lies the same fragility."*

Evelyn Marek watched from a distance, standing next to a trembling Amir Khaled. She clutched her notebook, a strange mix of awe and terror coursing through her.

"It's leaving," Amir said, his voice barely a whisper. "We should be running the opposite way, Evelyn."

"No," Evelyn replied, her gaze fixed on the towering entity. "It's not just a destroyer. It's learning. We need to know what it wants, or we'll never be able to stop it."

Amir shook his head in disbelief. "It's a walking apocalypse, and you want to study it?"

Evelyn didn't respond. She stepped forward, just enough to feel the edge of Chronovore's presence. "Chronovore!" she called out, her voice cutting through the howling wind.

The being paused, its tendrils retracting slightly as it turned toward her. "You persist," it said, its tone unreadable. "Why?"

"Because I want to understand," Evelyn said firmly. "You're not destroying everything outright. You're observing. Why?"

Chronovore's form shifted, its glowing core pulsing faintly. "You mortals have changed. Your world vibrates with progress and ruin, intertwined. I seek... context."

Amir whispered to Evelyn, "It's talking like it wants to take a stroll through a museum. This is insane."

Entering the City

Chronovore moved toward the distant glow of a modern city, a vast network of skyscrapers and bustling streets that radiated with light even in the darkness. As it approached, its tendrils brushed against abandoned outposts and scattered equipment left behind by fleeing dig teams, analyzing every fragment of this new world.

Its voice hummed with curiosity. "Metal towers reach for the heavens. Machines carry mortals across the earth. Yet their time remains finite. What purpose drives such fleeting creations?"

Evelyn and Amir followed from a distance in their vehicle, the hum of the engine barely audible against the desert wind.

"Do you think it's going to attack the city?" Amir asked, his knuckles white on the steering wheel.

"I don't know," Evelyn admitted. "But we have to see where this goes."

First Steps into Chaos

Chronovore's arrival in the city was met with panic. As its massive form entered the outskirts, cars skidded to a halt, horns blaring in a cacophony of chaos. People fled from the streets, abandoning markets and cafes as the alien entity loomed overhead.

Its tendrils extended, brushing against streetlights and buildings, absorbing the flow of electricity and the hum of human activity. The energy coursed through its form, distorting the air around it.

Inside a nearby control room, police officers stared at surveillance monitors, their faces pale. "What the hell is that thing?" one of them muttered.

"Whatever it is," another officer said, "it's not friendly. Get the evacuation protocols in place. Now!"

The Encounter with Humanity

Chronovore stopped in the center of a wide plaza, its core glowing brighter as it absorbed the frenetic energy of the city. Its tendrils reached toward digital billboards, flickering them into distorted chaos. Images of human achievements and advertisements played back at impossible speeds, fragments of speech and sound warping into a deafening hum.

Evelyn and Amir arrived on the scene just as armed personnel surrounded the entity, their weapons aimed but their hands trembling.

"Don't shoot!" Evelyn shouted, pushing her way through the barricade.

A soldier grabbed her arm. "Ma'am, you need to leave the area. Now."

"You don't understand!" Evelyn said, pulling free. "Shooting it will only make things worse."

Chronovore's tendrils coiled as it addressed the soldiers. "You point your tools of destruction at me? Your violence is meaningless."

The air grew heavy, and the soldiers staggered as their weapons aged rapidly, rusting and disintegrating in their hands. Panic erupted as they retreated, shouting orders to fall back.

"Stop!" Evelyn called out, stepping closer to Chronovore. "They don't understand you. Please, don't hurt them."

Chronovore paused, its core dimming slightly. "You speak as though their actions are not their own. Yet they act from fear. Fear leads to chaos."

Evelyn nodded. "And that's why you have to show them there's nothing to fear. If you destroy them, you'll only prove their fear right."

Chronovore's tendrils twitched, as though considering her words. "You advocate for them, mortal. Yet you know their fragility. Why?"

"Because we're more than our fear," Evelyn said. "We create. We learn. We grow."

Chronovore's voice softened, though it remained cold. "Then show me. Demonstrate this growth you speak of, or your species will end as so many others have."

The World Reacts

News of Chronovore's presence spread rapidly. Footage of the entity towering over the city played on screens around the globe, accompanied by speculation and fearmongering. Governments convened emergency meetings, debating whether to strike or negotiate.

In a high-security command center, General Marcus Harrington leaned over a conference table, his voice hard. "This thing is a threat. We can't sit back and let it destroy us."

A scientist at the table, Dr. Leah Kim, shook her head. "If we attack it, we risk provoking it. From what we've seen, it can manipulate time itself. Our weapons may be useless."

"Then what do you suggest?" Harrington demanded.

"Dr. Evelyn Marek," Kim said. "She's the only one who's made contact with it. She might be our best chance at understanding what it wants."

The Struggle for Balance

Chronovore moved through the city, its tendrils probing the infrastructure and its voice resonating in the air. "Your creations are numerous. Your ambitions vast. Yet your foundation is flawed. You build towers on sand, mortals. What prevents your collapse?"

Evelyn approached cautiously, her voice steady. "We're flawed, yes. But that's what makes us strive for something better. Progress comes from learning from our mistakes."

Chronovore's form pulsed with energy. "Progress? Or merely the illusion of it? You repeat the same patterns across time."

Evelyn hesitated, then stepped closer. "Maybe we do. But if you destroy us, you'll never see what we could become. Let us show you."

Chronovore's tendrils stilled. "Very well, mortal. You have intrigued me. But know this: your time is fleeting. Prove your worth, or I will bring an end to this chaos you call progress."

The Path Forward

As Chronovore continued its exploration, Evelyn realized the delicate balance she had to maintain. Humanity's survival now hinged on convincing an ancient, all-powerful entity that their existence had meaning. But with each passing moment, the world grew more fearful, and the line between observation and annihilation blurred.

"Amir," Evelyn said as they followed Chronovore from a distance, "we have to find a way to bridge the gap between its understanding and ours. If we can't..."

Amir nodded grimly. "Then it's the end of everything."

In the heart of the city, Chronovore loomed, its tendrils reaching outward as it absorbed the essence of a world vastly different from the one it had left behind. And for the first time in millennia, the being of time unbound found itself... questioning.

Chapter 16: The Hunt Begins
The World Reacts

The image of Chronovore towering over a modern city spread like wildfire. News broadcasts replayed the haunting footage: a massive, shadowy figure with tendrils of light and darkness warping the air around it, causing weapons to decay and time itself to stutter. Governments, intelligence agencies, and clandestine organizations all scrambled to respond.

In a war room buried deep beneath Washington, D.C., General Marcus Harrington stood before a screen displaying satellite footage of the creature.

"This thing isn't just a threat to a city," Harrington said, his voice hard and clipped. "It's a threat to the entire planet. If we don't act now, we may never get another chance."

Across the table, Dr. Leah Kim of the United Nations Science Coalition adjusted her glasses. "Act how, General? You saw what happened. Conventional weapons are useless. We don't even fully understand what we're dealing with."

Harrington slammed a hand on the table. "Then we make it our business to understand. Mobilize every asset we have—satellites, drones, research teams. Find its weaknesses. We don't have the luxury of waiting for it to decide to destroy us."

Dr. Kim shook her head, exasperated. "If you go in guns blazing, you risk provoking it into global annihilation. Have you considered talking to it?"

"Talking to it?" Harrington scoffed. "It's not a damn alien diplomat. It's a walking catastrophe."

A voice interrupted from the doorway. "Actually, General, it might be both."

All eyes turned to the speaker: an intelligence operative with a calm demeanor and an air of authority. "Agent Nolan West, CIA," he introduced himself, stepping into the room. "We've been monitoring the situation, and there's someone you'll want to speak to—Dr. Evelyn Marek. She's made direct contact with the entity and appears to have gained its trust."

Harrington frowned. "A scientist? She's not a soldier. She doesn't have the resources or expertise to handle this."

"Perhaps not," West conceded, "but she's alive, and her team survived the initial encounter. That's more than anyone else can say."

Evelyn Caught in the Crossfire

Meanwhile, Evelyn Marek and Amir Khaled had holed up in a safe house provided by their private benefactor. The desert city bustled outside their window, but inside, the air was heavy with tension. Evelyn sat at a cluttered desk, pouring over notes, maps, and ancient texts, while Amir paced nervously.

"You know they're coming for us, right?" Amir said, his voice filled with unease. "Governments, secret organizations—everyone who's seen that footage is going to want answers. And they're not going to ask nicely."

Evelyn didn't look up. "Let them come. They're not my priority."

Amir stopped pacing, staring at her incredulously. "Not your priority? Evelyn, they could label us as accomplices or terrorists for not warning them about Chronovore. Best case, we're interrogated for days. Worst case, we disappear."

Evelyn finally looked up, her green eyes sharp. "We're the only ones who can communicate with it, Amir. If the world starts shooting at Chronovore, we won't have to worry about interrogations because there won't be a world left."

Amir opened his mouth to argue but froze as his phone buzzed. He glanced at the screen, his face paling. "It's an unknown number."

"Don't answer it," Evelyn said immediately.

Before he could respond, the room's door burst open, and a team of armed operatives stormed inside. They moved with precision, weapons drawn but not fired. Agent Nolan West stepped in behind them, his calm expression betraying none of the tension in the room.

"Dr. Marek," he said evenly, "I believe you and I need to have a conversation."

The Global Hunt Begins

While Evelyn was taken into custody by the CIA, governments around the world activated their most secretive resources to locate and contain Chronovore.

In Moscow, a senior officer of the GRU watched a video feed of the creature disintegrating weapons in the hands of terrified soldiers. "Deploy Sentinel Program," he ordered. "If this thing can manipulate time, we'll use quantum disruptors to destabilize it."

In Beijing, scientists and military leaders huddled around a holographic projection of the creature. "Our satellites indicate its energy signature disrupts nearby technology," a scientist explained. "We've mobilized the Aurora Unit to counteract its influence with electromagnetic dampeners."

In a classified bunker beneath Geneva, a shadowy organization known only as *The Aegis* convened. Their leader, a sharp-featured woman named Dr. Isabelle Fontaine, addressed the council. "Chronovore is not a threat to a single nation—it's a threat to existence itself. We must act decisively. Initiate Protocol Eternity."

The Chase

Chronovore's journey through Earth's modern world was both destructive and exploratory. It moved from city to wilderness, observing humanity's creations and unraveling fragments of their history through the distortions of time it carried with it.

In a small European village, Chronovore's arrival caused clocks to spin backward, crops to wither and bloom in an instant, and people to experience fragmented memories of their ancestors. Its tendrils probed the ground, touching artifacts buried deep beneath the earth. A weathered man, trembling before the creature, whispered a prayer for salvation.

"Salvation is an illusion," Chronovore said, its voice a resonant hum. "Time consumes all. Yet you mortals persist in your fleeting constructs. Why?"

Elsewhere, drones shadowed the entity, their cameras capturing every movement. Chronovore, aware of the surveillance, reached out with a tendril, causing the drones to falter in midair, their footage glitching as though rewinding.

Back in a military command center, General Harrington slammed his fist on the table as the feed went dark. "It knows we're watching it! Damn it, can't we track this thing without losing assets?"

An analyst hesitated. "Sir, it's not just disrupting our equipment—it's actively manipulating the data. It's... playing with us."

The Interrogation

In a dimly lit interrogation room, Evelyn sat across from Agent West, her expression calm despite the circumstances. He placed a folder on the table, flipping it open to reveal satellite images of Chronovore's movements.

"You seem to have a unique relationship with this entity," West began. "Care to explain how that happened?"

"I don't have a relationship with it," Evelyn replied evenly. "I communicated with it because no one else could."

"Why you?" West pressed. "What makes you special?"

Evelyn leaned forward. "Because I treated it like an intelligence, not a monster. Chronovore doesn't care about our weapons or our power plays. It's trying to understand us."

West frowned. "And if it decides it doesn't like what it sees?"

Evelyn's voice softened. "Then nothing we do will stop it."

Tensions Rise

Chronovore continued to move across the globe, and the world's efforts to track and contain it grew increasingly frantic. Secret teams deployed experimental weapons and tactics, but every attempt to interfere was met with failure. The creature's ability to manipulate time rendered even the most advanced technologies useless.

At the same time, public fear reached a boiling point. Protests erupted, conspiracy theories flourished, and global leaders struggled to maintain order. Evelyn, now under constant surveillance, knew that the window for peaceful resolution was closing.

"Amir," she said one night, speaking to him through the glass of a CIA holding room, "we have to get back out there. If I can't convince Chronovore to stop, no one can."

Amir looked at her, his eyes weary but determined. "And if it doesn't listen?"

Evelyn's voice was firm. "Then we'll figure out another way. But we can't let the world destroy itself out of fear."

Chronovore's Declaration

In a remote mountain range, Chronovore stood atop a peak, its tendrils stretching toward the sky. Its voice resonated across the landscape, amplified by the temporal distortions it created.

"You mortals scramble like insects before the storm. Your fear is loud, but your wisdom is silent. Show me your worth, or I will bring an end to your chaos."

The world had heard its warning. The hunt had begun—but so had the countdown to humanity's reckoning.

Chapter 17: Unlocking Time
The Power Revealed

High in the snowy peaks of the Himalayas, Chronovore stood motionless, its shadowy form contrasting starkly against the blinding white landscape. Tendrils of shimmering energy extended outward, interacting with the frozen air and the mountain's ancient rocks. Time itself felt different here—sluggish, fractured, and tenuous.

Evelyn Marek and Amir Khaled, who had managed to negotiate their release under strict CIA surveillance, were observing from a safe distance, accompanied by Agent Nolan West and a team of heavily armed operatives.

"Evelyn," Amir whispered, his breath fogging in the cold air, "it's doing something. Something big."

Evelyn nodded, clutching her notebook tightly. "It's experimenting. Testing its abilities in a place where time feels... ancient."

Agent West frowned, his eyes narrowing behind his binoculars. "And what happens when it decides to test those abilities somewhere populated?"

Before anyone could answer, a deep, resonant hum filled the air, followed by a ripple that visibly distorted the space around Chronovore. The being's tendrils lashed out, and the landscape began to shift. Snow melted and froze again in seconds. Rocks cracked and reformed. Trees aged, grew, and withered in a matter of moments.

Amir gasped. "It's... rewinding time."

"No," Evelyn said, her voice trembling with awe. "It's *reshaping* it."

A Glimpse of the Past

Chronovore's core pulsed, and a massive tendril extended toward the mountainside. The snow and ice peeled away, revealing a lush, verdant forest where mammoths and saber-toothed tigers roamed freely. The air smelled of earth and wildflowers, a stark contrast to the icy cold moments before.

Agent West's radio crackled to life. "Command, you're not going to believe this," one of his operatives said, his voice tinged with disbelief. "We're looking at creatures that went extinct thousands of years ago."

Chronovore's voice boomed across the altered landscape. "The past is a memory written in the sands of time. Easily unearthed. Easily erased."

Evelyn stepped forward, ignoring West's attempt to hold her back. "Chronovore! Why are you doing this?"

The being turned toward her, its tendrils coiling like serpents. "To understand. Your kind clings to the past as though it defines you. Yet it is nothing but echoes. Observe."

With another pulse, Chronovore rewound further, the forest dissolving into an endless sea. Massive waves crashed against cliffs that no longer existed, and strange, primordial creatures swam through waters that hadn't been seen in eons.

Evelyn's breath caught. "This... this is the Earth millions of years ago."

Amir grabbed her arm, his voice panicked. "It's not just showing us, Evelyn. It's *changing* everything. What if it can't change it back?"

Chronovore tilted its form, as though considering Amir's words. "To change is to evolve. Fear of change binds your kind to stagnation. I am unbound."

The Future Unveiled

Without warning, the ripple reversed direction, and the landscape shifted once more. Snow and ice returned, but this time the mountaintop was no longer pristine. Skyscrapers rose where cliffs once stood, their metallic frames glowing faintly with blue light. Machines hovered in the air, moving in synchronized patterns.

Evelyn stared in awe. "This... this is Earth's future."

The team behind her was less impressed. "Is it still Earth?" one operative muttered, scanning the transformed terrain with suspicion.

Chronovore's tendrils reached toward the cityscape, drawing fragments of its existence closer. A hovering machine froze mid-flight, its form disassembling into a complex network of wires and circuits. The pieces rearranged themselves into an intricate pattern before dissolving into dust.

"Your future," Chronovore intoned, "is a construct of your choices. Fragile. Ephemeral. What value does progress hold if it ends in entropy?"

Evelyn stepped closer, her voice steady despite her racing heart. "You keep asking about value, meaning, purpose. But maybe those answers aren't in the past or the future. Maybe they're in the present—in what we do now."

Chronovore regarded her, its form flickering faintly. "Your present is fleeting, mortal. A blink in the vast continuum. What makes it significant?"

"Because it's *ours*," Evelyn said firmly. "It's the only moment we truly control."

The World Responds

As Chronovore continued its experiments, the ripple effects were felt globally. Clocks stopped and restarted erratically, entire regions experienced time distortions, and ancient ruins reappeared fully intact in some places while modern cities flickered as if they had never been built.

In a secure command center, General Harrington paced furiously. "We can't just sit here and watch this thing rewrite history and collapse the future! We need to act!"

Dr. Leah Kim, standing nearby, shook her head. "And what happens when your action accelerates the destruction, General? Chronovore is manipulating time on a scale we don't understand. Any interference could make things worse."

Harrington turned to Agent West, who had just returned from the field. "Your report says this scientist, Marek, is trying to reason with it. Do you honestly think that's a viable strategy?"

West shrugged. "It's worked so far. Chronovore hasn't destroyed us yet, and Marek seems to have its attention."

"That's not good enough," Harrington growled. "I want contingencies in place. If this thing becomes a clear threat, we take it out—whatever the cost."

The Human Connection

Back on the mountain, Evelyn pressed Chronovore further. "You've seen the past and the future, but neither seems to satisfy you. What are you really looking for?"

Chronovore's core pulsed, its tendrils retracting slightly. "I was created to impose order upon chaos. Yet in my observation, chaos persists. The past repeats. The future decays. Your existence is a paradox—resilient yet fragile. Explain this contradiction."

Evelyn took a deep breath. "We're not perfect. We make mistakes, but we learn from them. Our chaos isn't a flaw—it's what drives us to grow. You see entropy, but we see possibility."

Chronovore's tendrils stilled, the air around it vibrating with tension. "Possibility. A fleeting construct. Yet... intriguing."

It extended a tendril toward Evelyn, stopping inches from her face. She felt a surge of energy—memories flooding her mind, not her own but fragments of Earth's history and future. She gasped as she saw wars, triumphs, destruction, and rebirth.

"You allow chaos to define you," Chronovore said. "And yet you endure."

"Because chaos *is* life," Evelyn replied, her voice barely above a whisper.

A New Understanding

As Chronovore withdrew its tendrils, the distortions began to stabilize. The ancient past and distant future dissolved, leaving the mountain as it had been.

Evelyn turned to Amir, her expression resolute. "We need to show it that humanity isn't just chaos. We have to show it what makes us... us."

Amir frowned. "And how do you propose we do that? With a PowerPoint presentation?"

Evelyn smirked faintly. "No. With the truth."

Chronovore regarded them both, its voice softer now. "You claim meaning resides in your present. Then prove it. Show me the value of this fleeting moment."

The challenge had been set. Evelyn knew the stakes had never been higher. Chronovore's power to reshape time was both a gift and a curse, and the future of humanity depended on her ability to guide the ancient being toward understanding rather than annihilation.

Chapter 18: Symbiosis with Dr. Marek
The Edge of Despair

The bitter cold of the Himalayan night settled over the mountain, the sharp wind biting at Dr. Evelyn Marek's face. She huddled against a jagged rock formation, her breaths shallow and uneven. Around her, the world was unnervingly silent. The momentary stability Chronovore had granted by ceasing its temporal manipulations had left her and Amir stranded in an increasingly hostile environment.

"Amir," Evelyn whispered, her voice barely audible over the wind, "we can't stay here. The temperatures are dropping too fast."

Amir, huddled under a thin emergency blanket, nodded weakly. "You're right, but how exactly do we move? We're miles from the safe house, and that thing—" he gestured to Chronovore, which hovered ominously in the distance, "—doesn't seem interested in helping us."

Evelyn glanced at Chronovore, its tendrils slowly undulating as it observed the barren landscape. It had paused its relentless exploration, almost as though waiting for something.

She turned back to Amir, her voice trembling. "I don't think we have a choice anymore. If we want to survive, I have to try something... drastic."

Amir's eyes widened. "What do you mean, 'drastic'?"

Evelyn hesitated, her gaze locked on Chronovore. "I think... I think it wants more than just to understand us. It wants to experience us. It needs a host."

Amir recoiled, his expression a mix of horror and disbelief. "No. Absolutely not. Evelyn, bonding with that thing? It could kill you—or worse, take control."

"It's not ideal," Evelyn admitted, clutching her notebook tightly, "but it's our only chance. If I can show it what it means to be human, maybe I can convince it to spare us."

Amir shook his head, his voice rising. "And what if it decides you're not enough? What if it uses you to destroy the rest of us?"

Evelyn's eyes hardened. "If we do nothing, it'll destroy us anyway."

The Offer

Evelyn approached Chronovore cautiously, the frozen ground crunching beneath her boots. Its massive form turned toward her, tendrils retracting slightly as though acknowledging her presence.

"You persist," Chronovore said, its voice resonating through the air. "Even as your body weakens. Why do you not yield?"

Evelyn's voice was steady despite the fear clawing at her. "Because yielding isn't in our nature. We fight. We adapt. That's how we survive."

Chronovore's tendrils coiled tightly, the air around them rippling with energy. "Adaptation. A concept I observe but cannot embody. My essence is unbound by time, yet I am... disconnected."

Evelyn took a deep breath. "Then bond with me. See the world through my eyes. Feel what it means to be human."

Chronovore paused, its form flickering as though considering her words. "A symbiosis. Such a connection has not been attempted since my creation. The risk to you is significant."

Evelyn nodded. "I know the risks. But I also know that if we don't find a way to coexist, this ends in destruction—for both of us."

Amir, watching from a distance, shouted, "Evelyn, don't do this! There has to be another way!"

She turned to him, her expression resolute. "There isn't. Trust me, Amir."

The Bonding Process

Chronovore extended a single tendril toward Evelyn, its core pulsating with a faint, rhythmic glow. "Very well, mortal. I accept your offer. But understand this: our connection will be absolute. Your thoughts, your memories, your very essence will become part of me."

Evelyn stood her ground, her heart pounding in her chest. "I understand. Let's begin."

The tendril touched her forehead, and a surge of energy shot through her body. She gasped, her vision blurring as fragments of time and reality flooded her mind. Memories of Klyntar, of Chronovore's creation and betrayal, intertwined with her own. She saw her childhood, her struggles, her triumphs—all laid bare before the entity.

At the same time, Evelyn felt Chronovore's presence within her—a cold, alien intelligence probing her thoughts and emotions.

"You are... fragile," Chronovore said, its voice now echoing in her mind. "Yet your mind holds a resilience I did not anticipate."

Evelyn staggered but remained upright. "This is what it means to be human. Strength isn't just physical—it's emotional, mental."

The connection deepened, and Evelyn felt her body strengthen as Chronovore's energy flowed through her. She flexed her fingers, marveling at the newfound power coursing through her veins.

Amir approached cautiously, his face pale. "Evelyn? Are you... still you?"

She turned to him, her eyes glowing faintly with a golden light. "I'm still me," she said, her voice layered with an otherworldly resonance. "But now, I'm more."

A New Perspective

Through their bond, Chronovore began to experience the world in ways it never had. Emotions—raw, complex, and overwhelming—surged through its consciousness.

"What is this... ache?" Chronovore asked, its voice tinged with confusion.

"That's grief," Evelyn replied. "You're feeling my memories. The losses I've experienced."

"And this... warmth?"

"Love," she said softly. "The bond I share with those I care about."

Chronovore was silent for a moment, its presence within her shifting. "These sensations are... disorienting. They conflict with the logic of my existence."

"That's because being human isn't about logic," Evelyn said. "It's about connection. Relationships. Growth."

The First Test

Their conversation was interrupted by the distant sound of helicopters. A fleet of military aircraft appeared on the horizon, their lights piercing through the darkness. Evelyn's enhanced senses allowed her to hear the commands being issued.

"This is General Marcus Harrington," a voice boomed through a loudspeaker. "You are ordered to surrender immediately, or we will open fire."

Chronovore bristled within Evelyn, its energy flaring. "They seek to destroy us. Their fear blinds them."

"Wait," Evelyn said, holding up a hand. "Let me try."

She stepped forward, her glowing eyes fixed on the helicopters. "General Harrington!" she called out, her voice amplified by Chronovore's power. "You don't understand what you're dealing with. If you attack, you'll only make things worse."

The general's voice crackled through the speakers. "Dr. Marek? What the hell is going on? Are you... controlling that thing?"

"We've bonded," Evelyn explained. "It's trying to understand us, but you need to stand down. Provoking it could destroy everything."

"Bonded?" Harrington barked. "That's insane! You've made yourself a hostage!"

"Listen to me!" Evelyn shouted. "If you attack, we all lose. Stand down, and I'll work with you to find a solution."

There was a long pause before the general responded. "You've got one chance, Marek. But if that thing makes one wrong move, we're taking the shot."

The Uneasy Partnership

As the helicopters retreated, Evelyn turned to Amir, her expression weary but determined. "This is the only way forward. If we can show the world that Chronovore isn't just a destroyer, maybe we can stop the cycle of fear and violence."

Chronovore's voice echoed in her mind. "Your faith in your kind is... perplexing. Yet it intrigues me."

"Welcome to humanity," Evelyn said with a faint smile.

The bond was uneasy, fragile, and fraught with danger. But for the first time, Evelyn felt that there was hope—not just for survival, but for understanding. Together, she and Chronovore would navigate the precarious path between chaos and order, striving to prove that coexistence was possible.

Chapter 19: The Race for Control
The Secret Society Emerges

In the dimly lit chamber of an underground complex, high-ranking members of *The Aegis* gathered around a circular table. The room was adorned with ancient artifacts and modern technology, a juxtaposition of past and future reflecting the organization's singular goal: absolute control of the forces that shaped humanity.

At the head of the table, Dr. Isabelle Fontaine, the group's enigmatic leader, stood with her arms crossed. Her sharp, calculating gaze swept over the holographic projection of Chronovore, shimmering in the air above the table.

"This entity represents the pinnacle of our ambitions," Isabelle said, her voice calm yet commanding. "Time itself—raw, unbridled, and manipulable. If we can harness it, there is nothing we cannot achieve."

A younger man at the table, Marcus D'Arcy, frowned. "And if it refuses? Or worse, retaliates?"

Isabelle smirked. "Then we will take what we need by force. The bonding with Dr. Marek presents an unprecedented opportunity. Through her, we gain access to Chronovore's essence."

Another member, an older woman named Nadira, interjected. "She's a liability. Her moral compass will get in the way. If we move too aggressively, she could turn Chronovore against us."

Isabelle tapped a button on the table, and the hologram shifted to show Evelyn's glowing eyes and altered physiology during her symbiosis. "Then we give her a reason to comply. Retrieve her—and the creature."

Evelyn's New Reality

Far from the secretive machinations of *The Aegis*, Evelyn Marek sat at a temporary base in the shadow of the Himalayas. The bond with Chronovore had enhanced her perception; every tick of a clock and shift of the wind felt amplified. Yet, it also weighed on her mind.

Amir placed a steaming cup of tea in front of her. "You need to rest, Evelyn. Even with whatever superpowers that thing's giving you, you're still human."

Evelyn managed a weak smile. "Thanks, Amir. But I don't think rest is an option right now. Chronovore is still processing—"

"Processing?" Chronovore's voice resonated in her mind. *"Your world continues to unravel, yet you sit here."*

Evelyn flinched, closing her eyes. "We're regrouping. The governments are backing off for now, but that won't last long. And..." She hesitated.

Amir noticed. "And what?"

She sighed. "There's something else. I can feel it. A presence—watching us."

Amir frowned. "The military?"

Evelyn shook her head. "No. Something... older. More calculated."

The Aegis Strikes

Under cover of darkness, an elite strike team descended on the base. Equipped with state-of-the-art technology designed to disrupt temporal energy, the operatives moved with precision.

Inside, Evelyn's head snapped up, her glowing eyes narrowing. "They're here."

Amir glanced at her, startled. "Who?"

"An organized force," Chronovore replied within her. *"Driven by ambition, not survival. They seek to exploit."*

Evelyn stood, her body tense. "We need to move."

The first explosion rocked the building, shattering windows and plunging the base into chaos. Evelyn grabbed Amir's arm, pulling him toward an emergency exit. "Go! Get to the vehicle!"

"What about you?" Amir shouted over the noise.

Evelyn turned to face the incoming threat, her body radiating faint golden light. "I'll hold them off."

The Confrontation

As Evelyn stepped into the open, the strike team surrounded her, weapons raised. The leader, clad in sleek black armor with a glowing insignia of *The Aegis*, approached.

"Dr. Marek," the leader said, his voice distorted through a voice modulator, "we're not here to harm you. Come with us, and we can ensure your safety."

Evelyn's laugh was sharp, her voice carrying the resonance of Chronovore. "Safety? You blew up my base. Forgive me if I don't trust you."

The leader gestured, and his team activated devices that emitted a high-pitched whine. Evelyn felt Chronovore's energy falter slightly, its voice echoing in her mind.

"They have learned to disrupt my essence. Primitive, yet effective."

Evelyn gritted her teeth. "What do you want?"

The leader tilted his head. "Your symbiote. Its power is wasted on you. Give it to us willingly, and we will ensure its abilities are used to secure humanity's future."

"You mean control it," Evelyn shot back. "That's not happening."

The leader sighed. "Then I'm afraid we'll have to take it by force."

The Power of Symbiosis

As the strike team closed in, Evelyn felt Chronovore surge within her, its energy pushing past the disruptions. "You want it?" she said, her voice layered with Chronovore's. "Come and get it."

With a burst of golden light, Evelyn launched herself forward, her enhanced speed and strength catching the operatives off guard. She disarmed two of them in quick succession, their weapons crumbling to rust in her hands.

The leader barked orders. "Deploy temporal dampeners!"

Small devices were thrown into the air, emitting fields of shimmering energy. Evelyn staggered as Chronovore's presence within her wavered.

"They are clever," Chronovore admitted. *"But not clever enough."*

Tendrils of light extended from Evelyn's body, shattering the dampeners with precise strikes. She turned to the remaining operatives, her glowing eyes burning with defiance.

"This is your last chance," she said. "Leave, or I won't hold back."

The leader hesitated, then signaled a retreat. "This isn't over, Marek."

The Warning

As the strike team disappeared into the night, Evelyn collapsed to her knees, exhausted. Amir ran to her side, helping her up. "Are you okay?"

She nodded weakly. "I'm fine. But this is just the beginning. They'll be back—with more firepower."

Amir frowned. "Who *are* they?"

Evelyn's gaze hardened. "A secret society called *The Aegis*. They've been working in the shadows for centuries, waiting for something like Chronovore. And now that it's here, they won't stop until they control it."

Chronovore's voice rumbled within her. *"Control is an illusion. Their ambition will lead to their destruction."*

"Not if we stop them first," Evelyn replied aloud. She turned to Amir. "We need to move. If we're going to survive this—and keep Chronovore out of their hands—we need allies."

Amir raised an eyebrow. "Allies? Who do you have in mind?"

Evelyn looked out at the horizon, determination etched on her face. "Anyone who's willing to fight for humanity."

As dawn broke over the mountains, Evelyn knew the race for Chronovore's power had begun. But she also knew that to protect both humanity and the symbiote, she would have to outthink and outmaneuver an enemy willing to risk everything to claim the ultimate prize: control of time itself.

Chapter 20: A Glimpse into Eternity
The Accidental Catalyst

The Himalayan base was in shambles, its walls cracked and smoldering from the recent attack. Dr. Evelyn Marek sat cross-legged on the frozen ground, her breathing labored as Chronovore's energy coursed through her body. Amir Khaled stood nearby, pacing nervously as Evelyn struggled to stabilize their connection.

"Whatever you're doing," Amir said, his voice tinged with panic, "do it fast. If *The Aegis* comes back, we're done for."

Evelyn didn't respond, her focus entirely on the swirling mass of energy extending from her hands. Chronovore's voice echoed in her mind, a mix of curiosity and warning.

"You are attempting to grasp forces beyond your understanding, mortal."

"I don't have a choice," Evelyn muttered, sweat trickling down her face despite the freezing air. "We need to see what's coming. We need answers."

Chronovore's presence surged, filling her consciousness with a sensation both overwhelming and intoxicating. *"Very well. But know this: gazing into eternity reveals truths that cannot be unseen."*

As Chronovore's tendrils intertwined with her energy, the air around them began to shimmer. Time itself seemed to fracture, creating ripples that distorted the surrounding landscape. Rocks aged into dust and reformed; snow melted and froze in an instant.

Amir stopped pacing, his voice trembling. "Evelyn... what's happening?"

Evelyn's glowing eyes snapped open, and a pulse of golden light erupted from her body. "We're unlocking the future."

Visions of the Distant Future

The first vision hit them like a tidal wave. Evelyn and Chronovore were transported to a sprawling metropolis, its skyline dominated by towering structures of gleaming metal and glass. Vehicles hovered effortlessly above the streets, and artificial intelligences roamed freely among humans.

"This is Earth?" Evelyn asked, her voice echoing in the void surrounding her.

"A potential future," Chronovore replied, its voice calm but analytical. *"One of many paths."*

At first, the city appeared utopian, a harmonious blend of technology and nature. But as the vision deepened, cracks began to show. Fires raged in the outskirts, and robotic enforcers patrolled the streets with ruthless efficiency. People huddled in underground shelters, their faces hollow with fear.

Evelyn clenched her fists. "A dystopia hidden beneath a shiny exterior. Is this the result of humanity's obsession with control?"

Chronovore's tendrils pulsed faintly. *"It is one outcome. Progress leads to imbalance. Imbalance leads to collapse."*

The vision shifted abruptly, pulling them further into the timeline.

The Collapse of Civilization

They found themselves standing amidst a desolate wasteland. Skyscrapers lay in ruins, their metal skeletons jutting out of the sand like broken bones. The sky was an ominous shade of red, with ash swirling in the air.

Evelyn shuddered. "What happened here?"

Figures emerged from the haze—human survivors clad in makeshift armor, their faces gaunt and their eyes desperate. They fought over scraps of food, their movements wild and animalistic.

"This can't be us," Evelyn said, her voice cracking. "Not after everything we've achieved."

"Achievement breeds arrogance," Chronovore said. *"Arrogance blinds you to the cost of your actions."*

A monstrous figure appeared on the horizon, a twisted amalgamation of organic and mechanical parts. It roared, scattering the survivors. Evelyn felt a chill run through her. "What is that?"

"The result of your kind's hubris," Chronovore replied. *"An attempt to merge technology and biology, corrupted by desperation and greed."*

A Flicker of Hope

Before the despair of the wasteland could consume her, the vision shifted again. This time, Evelyn and Chronovore stood in a verdant landscape. The air was clean, and the sky was a brilliant blue. Communities thrived in harmony with nature, their structures made of sustainable materials and powered by renewable energy.

Children played in the fields, their laughter carrying on the wind. Adults worked together, tending to crops and sharing resources.

"This is..." Evelyn trailed off, her heart swelling with hope. "This is what we could be."

Chronovore's voice was softer now. *"An improbable outcome, yet not impossible. It requires balance—a balance your kind has seldom achieved."*

Evelyn turned to face the entity, her expression resolute. "Then we have to make this future a reality."

The Cataclysm of Eternity

The vision darkened once more, plunging them into an apocalyptic scene. The Earth itself seemed to writhe in agony as massive fissures split the ground, swallowing entire cities. The oceans boiled, and the atmosphere churned with violent storms.

Evelyn covered her face as a deafening roar echoed through the chaos. Above them, Chronovore—vast and unbound—loomed over the destruction, its tendrils tearing through time and space.

"That's... you," Evelyn whispered, horrified.

"It is a possibility," Chronovore admitted. *"If your kind fails to guide me, I may fulfill the purpose for which I was created: to unmake chaos by consuming it."*

Evelyn stepped forward, her voice rising above the noise. "No! That's not who you are anymore. You don't have to follow that path."

"And yet the choice may not be mine alone," Chronovore replied. *"You wield influence, but humanity's collective will shapes its fate."*

Returning to the Present

The visions dissolved, and Evelyn found herself back on the icy mountainside, gasping for breath. Amir was at her side, shaking her shoulder. "Evelyn! Are you okay?"

She nodded weakly, her mind reeling from what she had seen. "I'm fine. But we have to act, Amir. We've seen what's at stake."

Amir frowned. "What did you see?"

Evelyn's glowing eyes met his. "Everything. The rise and fall of humanity. The best and worst of what we can be. And..." She hesitated, her voice trembling. "I saw what happens if we fail to guide Chronovore."

Amir's face paled. "And if we succeed?"

Evelyn placed a hand on his shoulder, her resolve hardening. "Then we have a chance to create something better."

The Warning

Chronovore's voice echoed in her mind as she stood. *"You have glimpsed eternity, but the future is not fixed. Choices must be made. Paths must be forged."*

Evelyn turned her gaze toward the horizon, her heart heavy yet determined. "Then we'll make the right choices. Together."

The weight of the visions lingered, a constant reminder of the stakes. The potential for hope or despair rested on the edge of every decision they would make from that moment forward. And with Chronovore at her side, Evelyn knew the race to secure humanity's future had only just begun.

Chapter 21: Betrayal in the Shadows
The Uneasy Calm

Days after the catastrophic visions of Earth's potential futures, Dr. Evelyn Marek and Amir Khaled sat in a dimly lit safe house deep within a bustling city. Their temporary sanctuary was surrounded by towering skyscrapers and the hum of urban life, but Evelyn could not shake the oppressive weight of what she had seen.

"You've been quiet," Amir said, breaking the silence as he sipped from a steaming mug of tea. "Quieter than usual, I mean."

Evelyn looked up from her notebook, where sketches of Chronovore's tendrils and temporal symbols filled the pages. "I'm trying to figure out the next step," she said. "We can't afford to stay still. The Aegis is closing in, and the governments aren't far behind."

Amir set his mug down, leaning forward. "We need allies, Evelyn. Someone we can trust."

She nodded. "Agreed. But trust is a commodity in short supply right now."

At that moment, a knock echoed through the room. Evelyn and Amir exchanged a glance, their expressions wary. Amir grabbed a knife from the table and approached the door. "Who is it?"

"It's me," came a familiar voice. Evelyn immediately recognized it as Marcus Reid, an old colleague and archaeologist who had helped her piece together the first fragments of the Pyramid of Eternity's location.

Amir hesitated, looking at Evelyn. "Should we trust him?"

Evelyn frowned but nodded. "Marcus has always been loyal. Let him in."

Amir unlocked the door, and Marcus stepped inside, his face pale and lined with worry. He carried a satchel and looked around nervously before speaking. "You don't have much time. The Aegis is onto you."

The False Warning

Marcus sat across from Evelyn, placing his satchel on the table. "I intercepted some chatter. They know you're here, Evelyn. They're planning a coordinated strike."

Evelyn narrowed her eyes, studying his face. "How do you know that? You haven't been in contact with me for months."

Marcus hesitated, his fingers fidgeting with the strap of his satchel. "I've been keeping tabs on *The Aegis*. When I heard your name linked to Chronovore, I knew they'd come after you. I couldn't just stand by."

Amir crossed his arms, still holding the knife. "Why didn't you warn us earlier? And how do we know you're not leading them straight to us?"

Marcus leaned forward, his voice earnest. "Because I owe you, Evelyn. You trusted me when no one else did. I'd never betray that."

Evelyn sighed, rubbing her temples. "If they're closing in, we need to move. Did you bring anything useful?"

Marcus nodded, opening his satchel to reveal maps and documents. "These are schematics for an old underground tunnel network nearby. It'll get you out of the city undetected."

Evelyn studied the documents, her brow furrowing. "This... this could work."

Amir remained skeptical. "Or it could be a trap."

Evelyn glanced at Marcus, her voice firm. "Is it?"

Marcus met her gaze, his expression steady. "No."

The Betrayal Unfolds

As night fell, Evelyn, Amir, and Marcus moved toward the tunnel entrance marked on the map. Chronovore remained dormant within Evelyn, its presence a faint hum in her mind.

"Your trust is misplaced," Chronovore's voice echoed in her thoughts.

"What do you mean?" Evelyn whispered, careful not to alert the others.

"The one you call Marcus conceals duplicity. Observe his movements."

Evelyn glanced at Marcus, who walked ahead with an unusual stiffness. Her instincts, sharpened by her bond with Chronovore, began to scream that something was wrong.

"Marcus," she said cautiously, "why are you so eager to help us? What's in this for you?"

Marcus stopped, turning to face her. His expression hardened. "It's nothing personal, Evelyn. But Chronovore is too powerful to be left with you. The Aegis has plans for it—plans that could change everything."

Amir's hand darted toward his knife, but Marcus was faster. He pulled a small device from his pocket and pressed a button. A high-pitched frequency filled the air, and Evelyn cried out as Chronovore's energy recoiled within her.

Amir lunged at Marcus, but two armed operatives emerged from the shadows, guns trained on him. "Don't move," one of them barked.

"You sold us out," Evelyn said through gritted teeth, struggling to stay upright as the frequency disrupted her bond with Chronovore.

Marcus stepped closer, his tone regretful but resolute. "You don't understand what's at stake, Evelyn. The Aegis isn't just another shadow organization. They want to use Chronovore to rewrite history—to fix humanity's mistakes."

Evelyn glared at him. "You think rewriting history will fix anything? You'll just create new problems. You're playing with forces you don't understand."

Marcus sighed. "Maybe. But at least we'll have control."

The Desperate Escape

As Marcus and his operatives prepared to take Evelyn into custody, Chronovore's voice surged in her mind, overpowering the pain.

"You are resilient, mortal. Use my strength."

Evelyn's eyes glowed fiercely as Chronovore's tendrils erupted from her body, shattering the device Marcus had activated. The operatives opened fire, but the bullets disintegrated mid-air as Chronovore's energy warped time around them.

Marcus stumbled back, his face pale. "You don't understand! If you don't let us take it, *The Aegis* will come for you with everything they have!"

Evelyn advanced on him, her voice resonating with Chronovore's power. "Let them try."

Amir tackled one of the operatives, disarming him with a swift strike. He turned to Evelyn, shouting, "We need to go—now!"

Evelyn nodded, her tendrils retracting as she grabbed Marcus's satchel. "You're not worth killing," she told Marcus coldly. "But if you come after us again, you won't get a second chance."

With that, she and Amir disappeared into the darkness of the tunnel network.

The Fallout

As they emerged from the tunnels hours later, Evelyn leaned against a wall, exhausted. Amir handed her a canteen of water, his expression grim. "We can't keep running like this. They'll find us again."

Evelyn took a sip, her hands trembling. "Then we need to go on the offensive. Find out where *The Aegis* is operating and shut them down."

Amir raised an eyebrow. "How do you plan to do that?"

Evelyn held up the satchel she'd taken from Marcus. "He gave us more than he realized. This has everything we need to turn the tables."

Chronovore's voice rumbled in her mind. *"Betrayal breeds clarity. Your path is now illuminated."*

Evelyn straightened, her resolve hardening. "Then it's time to stop running. If they want a fight, we'll give them one."

The betrayal had shaken her, but it also strengthened her resolve. With Chronovore's power and the stolen intel, Evelyn knew she had the tools to strike back. The question now was whether she could stay one step ahead of the shadows closing in around her.

Chapter 22: The Nexus Point
The Call of the Nexus

The morning sky above the dense Amazon rainforest was a kaleidoscope of gold and green, with beams of sunlight piercing through the thick canopy. Dr. Evelyn Marek and Amir Khaled trudged through the humid jungle, their clothes damp with sweat and their nerves frayed from constant vigilance.

Chronovore had grown restless within Evelyn, its presence vibrating at an intensity she hadn't felt before. The creature was drawn to something—a source of energy unlike anything they had encountered.

Amir wiped his brow, glancing at Evelyn as they paused on a ridge overlooking the vast expanse of trees. "Are you going to tell me where we're going? Or is this another one of your 'I'll know when I see it' situations?"

Evelyn adjusted her backpack, her glowing eyes scanning the horizon. "Chronovore is pulling us toward something... powerful. It's not entirely clear, but it's near. We're close."

Amir frowned. "And this thing you're chasing, is it going to help us, or are we walking into another disaster?"

Before Evelyn could answer, Chronovore's voice resonated within her mind. *"A nexus lies ahead—a convergence of temporal energies. It is both a source of great potential and an engine of destruction."*

Evelyn relayed the message to Amir, her voice steady but cautious. "It's a temporal nexus. A point where time intersects and overlaps. If Chronovore is right, it could amplify its powers exponentially—but it could also destabilize everything."

Amir's eyes widened. "You mean... destroy time itself?"

Evelyn nodded grimly. "If we're not careful."

The Discovery

Hours later, they stumbled upon an ancient ruin hidden beneath layers of moss and vines. Massive stone pillars rose from the ground, etched with symbols that seemed to shimmer and shift when viewed from different angles.

"This is it," Evelyn whispered, awe and trepidation mingling in her voice.

As they stepped closer, Chronovore's energy surged within her, manifesting faint tendrils of light around her hands. *"The nexus sleeps but stirs in my presence. It recognizes me."*

Amir ran a hand over one of the stone carvings, his voice tinged with curiosity. "These markings... they're not just ancient—they're alien. This is connected to your Pyramid of Eternity, isn't it?"

Evelyn nodded, crouching to examine the central altar. "The nexus must have been created by the same civilization that imprisoned Chronovore. They understood temporal energy in ways we're only beginning to comprehend."

Suddenly, the air grew heavy, and the ground beneath their feet trembled. A low hum filled the ruin, and faint arcs of light began to dance between the pillars.

Amir took a step back. "Uh, Evelyn? I think you woke it up."

Evelyn stood, her glowing eyes narrowing. "No. *We* didn't. Chronovore did."

The creature's voice echoed outward now, audible to both of them. *"The nexus resonates with my essence. It remembers its purpose."*

The Nexus Activates

As the energy intensified, the ruin transformed. The symbols on the pillars illuminated, and a vortex of swirling light formed above the central altar. Evelyn and Amir shielded their eyes as the nexus roared to life, its power warping the very fabric of reality around them.

Fragments of the past and future flickered in the air—prehistoric beasts roaming the jungle, towering cities rising and falling, and unfamiliar stars shining in alien skies.

Amir stared in stunned silence. "What... what are we looking at?"

Evelyn's voice was hushed, her awe evident. "Time itself. The nexus is showing us the timeline—fractured, overlapping, infinite."

Chronovore's tendrils extended from Evelyn, reaching toward the vortex. *"With this power, I can transcend all limitations. I will become one with eternity."*

Evelyn's heart raced. "Wait, Chronovore. If you merge with the nexus, you could destabilize everything. You said it yourself—it's dangerous."

"Danger is irrelevant," Chronovore replied. *"Through the nexus, I can impose order upon chaos. I can rewrite the errors of existence."*

Amir stepped forward, panic in his voice. "Evelyn, stop it! If it taps into that thing, who knows what will happen?"

Evelyn raised her hands, her voice firm. "Chronovore, listen to me. You don't need to rewrite everything. You've seen what happens when we try to control time—it leads to destruction."

Chronovore hesitated, its tendrils retracting slightly. *"Your resistance is illogical. The nexus is a tool of perfection."*

Evelyn's voice softened. "No, it's a weapon. One that could destroy everything you've observed, everything you've tried to understand. Is that what you want?"

The Unexpected Threat

Before Chronovore could respond, a sharp sound pierced the air—a high-pitched frequency similar to the one used by *The Aegis*. Evelyn staggered, clutching her head as Chronovore recoiled within her.

From the shadows, armed operatives emerged, led by Dr. Isabelle Fontaine. She smiled coldly as her team surrounded the ruin, each operative carrying devices designed to disrupt Chronovore's energy.

"You've done all the hard work for us, Dr. Marek," Isabelle said, her voice smooth and confident. "Finding the nexus was no small feat, but now it's time for you to step aside."

Amir glared at her. "You're insane. Do you have any idea what you're messing with?"

Isabelle raised an eyebrow. "Of course. That's why we're here—to harness its potential for humanity's benefit."

Evelyn straightened, despite the pain coursing through her. "You mean to control it. But you don't understand the consequences. The nexus isn't stable. If you tamper with it—"

"We'll secure it," Isabelle interrupted, her tone sharp. "And we'll do it without your interference."

She gestured, and her operatives activated more disruption devices. The nexus flickered, its energy faltering. Chronovore writhed within Evelyn, its voice strained. *"They weaken me... and the nexus."*

Evelyn's glowing eyes blazed. "You'll destroy us all!"

The Desperate Gamble

As the nexus began to destabilize, arcs of wild energy lashed out, tearing through the ruins and the surrounding jungle. Operatives scrambled for cover as reality itself seemed to fracture, moments of the past and future bleeding into the present.

Evelyn turned to Amir. "We have to stop them!"

"And how do we do that?" Amir shouted, dodging a crackling bolt of energy.

Evelyn closed her eyes, reaching deep into her bond with Chronovore. "Trust me."

She stepped forward, her body radiating light as she addressed Chronovore. "You said the nexus remembers you. That means you can stabilize it. Use its power to restore balance—but don't merge with it. Let it remain dormant."

Chronovore's voice was hesitant. *"The risk is great. Failure will annihilate all timelines."*

"And success?" Evelyn asked.

"Stability. But the nexus's power will remain beyond reach."

Evelyn nodded. "Then do it. Prove that chaos can coexist with order."

The Balance Restored

With a final surge of effort, Chronovore extended its tendrils into the nexus. The swirling vortex roared louder, then slowly began to stabilize. The wild energy receded, and the temporal fractures healed.

Dr. Fontaine screamed at her operatives. "Stop her! Don't let them take control!"

Amir tackled one of the operatives, disarming him, while Evelyn stood firm, her connection with Chronovore unshakable.

The nexus pulsed one final time before going dormant, its light fading into the stone. The ruins fell silent, leaving only the hum of Chronovore's presence within Evelyn.

Isabelle glared at Evelyn, her face twisted with fury. "You've ruined everything!"

"No," Evelyn said calmly. "I saved it."

The Aftermath

As Fontaine and her team retreated, Evelyn and Amir stood amidst the ruins, their breaths heavy with exhaustion.

Amir looked at her, his face a mix of relief and awe. "You did it. You actually did it."

Evelyn nodded, her voice quiet. "For now. But this isn't over. The nexus is dormant, but it's still here. And so are the people who want to exploit it."

Chronovore's voice echoed in her mind, steady and resolute. *"Balance has been preserved. But the struggle continues. You have chosen wisely... this time."*

Evelyn glanced at the horizon, the weight of her choices pressing heavily on her. "Let's hope we keep making the right ones."

Chapter 23: A Battle Through Time
The Converging Forces

The ruins of the temporal nexus buzzed with a dangerous energy, the hum reverberating through the dense jungle like a living heartbeat. Dr. Evelyn Marek stood at the edge of the ancient site, her glowing eyes scanning the horizon. Beside her, Amir Khaled adjusted his gear nervously, the tension palpable.

"They're coming, aren't they?" Amir asked, gripping a makeshift weapon he'd scavenged from earlier skirmishes.

Evelyn nodded, her voice quiet but resolute. "The Aegis won't stop until they have the nexus. And they won't be the only ones. We're standing in front of the most dangerous power source on Earth."

Amir chuckled nervously. "Great. We've got front-row seats to the end of the world."

Chronovore's voice resonated in Evelyn's mind, calm and calculating. *"Your enemies are many, their intentions divergent. They will bring chaos to the nexus, further destabilizing its delicate balance."*

Evelyn glanced at the glowing symbols on the nexus pillars, feeling the immense energy pulsating beneath her feet. "We can't let them activate it. If the nexus fractures, it'll scatter time itself—different eras bleeding into each other. It'll be chaos."

Amir sighed, his grip tightening on his weapon. "So, what's the plan? Because I'm guessing 'wing it' isn't going to cut it this time."

Evelyn's gaze hardened. "We hold them off. We keep them from the nexus at all costs. And if it comes down to it..." She trailed off, unwilling to voice the worst-case scenario.

Amir frowned but didn't press her. "Got it. Fight now, panic later."

The Battle Begins

The first assault came at sunrise. Helicopters roared over the jungle canopy, their blades slicing through the air. Ropes dropped, and heavily armed operatives descended with precision. At the same time, rogue factions surged from the jungle—mercenaries, rival scientists, and even a few rogue soldiers who had defected for a chance to claim the nexus's power.

Evelyn and Amir ducked behind a crumbled pillar as bullets ricocheted around them.

"Well, they didn't waste any time," Amir muttered, pulling Evelyn down as a grenade exploded nearby.

Evelyn peeked out, her glowing eyes locking onto the central altar. The nexus's energy was reacting to the chaos, the swirling light above it growing brighter and more unstable.

"This is exactly what we can't let happen," Evelyn said, her voice tense.

She raised her hand, and Chronovore's tendrils erupted from her body, lashing out at the nearest attackers. A group of mercenaries fired at her, but the bullets disintegrated mid-air as the tendrils warped time around them.

Amir took the opportunity to charge another operative, disarming him with a swift move. "One down, a hundred to go," he muttered.

Temporal Chaos Unleashed

As the battle raged, a group of operatives reached the central altar. One of them, clad in black armor bearing *The Aegis* insignia, activated a device that pulsed with a sharp, high-pitched frequency.

Evelyn felt a jolt of pain as the frequency disrupted her bond with Chronovore. "They're trying to force the nexus open!" she shouted.

The nexus roared in response, its energy surging uncontrollably. Temporal distortions rippled outward, and the world around them began to shift.

Evelyn and Amir staggered as the jungle dissolved into a barren desert. Massive, prehistoric creatures roamed in the distance, their roars echoing through the air.

"Is that... a dinosaur?" Amir asked, his voice filled with disbelief.

Before Evelyn could respond, another ripple shifted them again. Now they stood amidst a medieval battlefield. Knights in gleaming armor clashed with futuristic mercenaries, their swords meeting plasma rifles in a surreal spectacle.

"This is what happens when time fractures," Evelyn said, her voice grim. "Everything starts bleeding together."

Battling Across Eras

The temporal chaos grew worse with each passing moment. Evelyn and Amir were thrown from one era to another, battling their enemies in wildly different environments.

In one moment, they were surrounded by Roman soldiers in a grand coliseum. Evelyn deflected a spear with a burst of Chronovore's energy, while Amir grabbed a shield and fended off attackers.

In the next instant, they found themselves in the trenches of World War I. Bombs exploded overhead, and the sky was filled with the deafening roar of airplanes. Evelyn used Chronovore's tendrils to shield them from shrapnel as they pushed toward a glowing rift in the distance.

Through it all, their enemies pursued them relentlessly. Dr. Isabelle Fontaine appeared time and again, her operatives adapting to each new environment with unnerving efficiency.

"You can't run forever, Marek!" Fontaine shouted, her voice cutting through the chaos.

Evelyn turned, her glowing eyes blazing. "I'm not running—I'm stopping this!"

The Final Push

The last distortion brought them to a futuristic cityscape, its towering skyscrapers glowing with neon lights. Hovering vehicles zipped through the air, and robotic enforcers patrolled the streets. The nexus's core hovered above the city, its energy pulsating violently.

Fontaine and her remaining operatives appeared moments later, now armed with advanced weapons scavenged from the future.

"This ends here," Fontaine said, leveling her weapon at Evelyn.

Evelyn stepped forward, Chronovore's energy swirling around her. "You don't understand what you're tampering with, Fontaine. If the nexus collapses, it'll destroy all timelines—including yours."

Fontaine smirked, unfazed. "Then I'll rebuild them the way they should have been."

Evelyn raised her hands, and Chronovore's tendrils lashed out, intercepting Fontaine's weapon as she fired. The blast ricocheted, striking a nearby structure and causing it to collapse.

Amir tackled an operative, disarming him with a swift move. "Evelyn, we don't have much time!"

Evelyn turned to the nexus's core, her expression resolute. "Chronovore, we have to stabilize it. Can you do it?"

"It will require complete synchronization," Chronovore replied. *"But the risk is great. Failure will unmake us both."*

Evelyn nodded. "Then let's do it."

Stabilizing the Nexus

As Fontaine's forces closed in, Evelyn stepped toward the nexus's core. Chronovore's energy surged, intertwining with the unstable rift. The core roared in protest, its wild energy lashing out in every direction.

Fontaine screamed in frustration. "Stop her!"

Evelyn ignored her, focusing entirely on the connection. "Amir, hold them off!"

Amir gritted his teeth, using everything at his disposal to keep the attackers at bay. "No pressure or anything, Evelyn!"

The nexus's energy intensified, threatening to overwhelm Evelyn. But with Chronovore's guidance, she began to stabilize the core. The wild distortions slowed, the overlapping eras fading away.

Finally, with a deafening roar, the core pulsed one last time before going dormant. The ruins returned to their original state, silent and still.

The Aftermath

Evelyn collapsed to her knees, her body trembling from exhaustion. Amir rushed to her side, helping her up. "You did it," he said, his voice filled with awe.

Fontaine stood nearby, her face twisted with fury. "You think this is over?" she spat. "You can't protect the nexus forever."

Evelyn straightened, her glowing eyes meeting Fontaine's. "Watch me."

As Fontaine retreated with her remaining forces, Evelyn and Amir sat amidst the ruins, the weight of their journey pressing heavily on them.

"What now?" Amir asked.

Evelyn looked toward the horizon, determination burning in her eyes. "We find a way to keep it safe. For good. And we prepare for whatever comes next."

Chronovore's voice echoed in her mind, steady and resolute. *The battle is won, but the war for time is eternal. Choose your allies wisely, mortal. The future depends on it.*

Evelyn nodded. "Then we'll make sure the right future wins."

Chapter 24: The Final Seal
The Weight of the Decision

The ruins of the temporal nexus lay silent, their once-vibrant energies now dormant but far from extinguished. Dr. Evelyn Marek sat on the crumbled remains of a stone altar, her hands trembling as she turned the pages of her notebook. Her glowing eyes, a constant reminder of her bond with Chronovore, reflected the dim light of the setting sun.

Amir Khaled stood nearby, leaning against a pillar with his arms crossed. His face was a mixture of exhaustion and concern. "You've been staring at that notebook for hours. What's the plan?"

Evelyn didn't look up. Her voice was soft, almost fragile. "I'm not sure there is one. Not this time."

Amir frowned. "That's not like you. You always have a plan—some crazy, barely-holding-it-together plan, but still."

She finally met his gaze, and the weariness in her expression sent a chill down his spine. "This isn't just another challenge, Amir. This is *everything.*"

Chronovore's voice echoed in her mind, calm but insistent. *"The nexus is stable for now, but it remains vulnerable. As long as I exist, others will seek to exploit me. You must choose how this ends."*

Evelyn closed her notebook, staring at the glowing nexus core. "That's what I'm afraid of."

Chronovore's Plea

Later that night, as the stars pierced the jungle canopy, Evelyn sat alone near the nexus. Amir had fallen asleep nearby, his exhaustion finally catching up to him. Chronovore's presence pulsed faintly within her, a constant companion in her thoughts.

"You hesitate," Chronovore said.

"Of course I do," Evelyn replied aloud, her voice a whisper. "You're asking me to decide the fate of the world—and you."

"You have seen what I am capable of," Chronovore continued. *"I am a force beyond your comprehension. Yet I am not bound by destruction. I can learn. I can adapt."*

Evelyn shook her head, frustration rising in her chest. "And what if you don't? What if you decide humanity isn't worth saving? You've seen how flawed we are."

"Flawed, yes. But resilient. I have witnessed your kind endure chaos, adapt to it, even thrive within it. That is why I chose to bond with you."

Her voice cracked. "And if I make the wrong choice? If I let you stay free and it all falls apart?"

"Then it will fall," Chronovore admitted. *"But you must also ask: what is lost if you seal me away? What potential is buried alongside your fear?"*

Amir's Argument

The following morning, Evelyn explained the dilemma to Amir. His reaction was immediate and fiery.

"You're even *considering* keeping it free?" he said, pacing back and forth. "This is Chronovore we're talking about. The same entity that nearly unraveled time, wiped out civilizations, and could do it all again in the blink of an eye."

Evelyn stood, her expression defensive. "And yet it didn't. It's been with me through everything, Amir. It's helped us, saved us more times than I can count. Doesn't that mean something?"

"Sure," Amir shot back. "It means it knows it needs you. But what happens when it doesn't? When it decides it's done learning and starts dictating? You think you can control something like that forever?"

Evelyn's voice rose. "It's not about control! It's about trust!"

Amir stopped, his eyes narrowing. "Trust? You're talking about trusting a being that exists outside time, that sees us as fleeting moments in its endless existence. Evelyn, you can't trust something like that."

She hesitated, her resolve wavering. "Maybe I can't. But if we seal it away again, we're no better than the ones who created it. We're just running from a problem instead of facing it."

Amir softened slightly but shook his head. "Sometimes, running is the smart choice."

The Final Test

Evelyn approached the nexus core, its faint glow casting long shadows across the ruins. Chronovore's presence loomed within her, a steady hum of energy that filled her mind.

"You are ready," Chronovore said. *"Your decision will shape not only this moment but the course of your kind's existence."*

She placed her hands on the glowing altar, feeling the weight of its power resonate through her. Memories flooded her mind—her first encounter with Chronovore, the battles they had fought together, the glimpses of potential futures.

"You've seen everything we arc," Evelyn said. "Our worst and our best. If I let you stay free, can you promise me you'll choose the latter?"

Chronovore was silent for a moment, its presence contemplative. *"I cannot promise. But I can strive. I can learn."*

Tears welled in her eyes. "That's not good enough."

"It is the only truth I can give you," Chronovore replied. *"A promise from a being bound by time is fleeting. I exist beyond such constraints. But in you, I have found purpose. If you allow it, I will continue to seek understanding."*

The Decision

Amir stood behind her, his voice tense. "Evelyn, whatever you're doing, do it now. I can't stay here, watching you gamble with everything."

Evelyn turned to face him, her glowing eyes meeting his. "I have to believe in something, Amir. And right now, I believe in Chronovore."

Amir's jaw tightened, but he nodded reluctantly. "Then let's hope you're right."

She turned back to the nexus and took a deep breath. Her hands pressed against the glowing core, and Chronovore's energy surged through her.

"I am yours," Chronovore said. *"Together, we will shape what comes next."*

The nexus pulsed, and the glow around it dimmed. The ancient energy receded, sealing itself into a dormant state. Chronovore remained within Evelyn, its power now intertwined with hers, but the nexus itself was protected—silent and unreachable to those who sought to exploit it.

Aftermath

The jungle was quiet as Evelyn and Amir left the ruins, the weight of their journey pressing heavily on them.

"Do you think we made the right choice?" Amir asked, his voice hesitant.

Evelyn glanced at him, her expression unreadable. "I don't know. But for now, we've bought humanity a chance. What we do with it... that's up to us."

Chronovore's voice echoed softly in her mind. *"Your choice was bold. Now, we see what it brings."*

As they disappeared into the trees, the ruins of the nexus faded into the background, a silent testament to the fragile balance between chaos and order—and the choices that define the future.

Chapter 25: Eternal Wanderer
A World Left Behind

The sun cast its golden glow over the dense jungle, the ruins of the nexus now quiet and dormant. Dr. Evelyn Marek stood on the edge of the site, the weight of her decision pressing heavily on her. Chronovore's presence within her had grown quiet, almost contemplative, but she could still feel its immense power coursing through her—a reminder of the fragile balance they had struck.

Amir Khaled approached from behind, his footsteps soft but deliberate. "You've been staring at that thing for hours," he said, nodding toward the nexus. "What are you thinking?"

Evelyn turned to face him, her expression a mixture of exhaustion and resolution. "That this is only the beginning."

Amir crossed his arms, his brow furrowed. "You mean for Chronovore?"

"For all of us," Evelyn replied. "The world's not going to stop coming after this power. And Chronovore... it's more than just a force. It's something the world isn't ready for."

Amir sighed, leaning against a nearby pillar. "So what do we do now? Keep running? Keep fighting? There's only so much we can do, Evelyn."

She shook her head. "No. Running isn't the answer anymore. And neither is fighting. Chronovore needs freedom— not just from the nexus, but from me. From all of this."

The Farewell

As the jungle settled into a hushed stillness, Evelyn closed her eyes and reached inward, where Chronovore's energy pulsed faintly in her mind.

"You have made your decision," Chronovore said, its voice resonating softly.

"I have," Evelyn whispered. "You've seen everything we are—our flaws, our strengths. If you stay here, the world will never let you exist in peace. But out there..." She gestured toward the sky. "You can find your own path."

Amir stepped closer, his voice tinged with concern. "You're... letting it go? Evelyn, are you sure that's a good idea?"

Evelyn turned to him, her glowing eyes meeting his. "It's the only idea. Chronovore isn't just a weapon or a threat. It's something greater, something we can't fully understand. And if it stays tethered to us, it'll never have the chance to figure out what it's meant to be."

Amir hesitated, then nodded slowly. "If anyone can make this work, it's you. But... how do you even let go of something like that?"

The Release

Evelyn stepped into the center of the nexus, the faint glow of its dormant energy reflecting off her skin. She placed her hands on the ancient altar, her breath steady as she focused on the bond she shared with Chronovore.

"You believe I must leave," Chronovore said. *"Yet you also fear what I may become without you."*

"You're right," Evelyn admitted. "But that's what trust is, isn't it? Letting go, even when it's terrifying. I have to believe in you, just like you believed in me."

Chronovore's energy surged briefly, a warm, comforting pulse that filled her mind. *"You have shown me what it means to exist beyond purpose. To learn, to adapt, to grow. I will honor that gift."*

The air around them shifted as Chronovore began to withdraw its essence from her. Evelyn gasped, feeling the immense power recede, leaving her body lighter yet profoundly empty. Tendrils of shimmering light emerged from her chest, spiraling upward toward the sky.

Amir shielded his eyes as the tendrils coalesced into a glowing form above the nexus—a swirling, radiant figure that pulsed with infinite potential.

Evelyn looked up, tears streaming down her face. "Chronovore... thank you."

"No," it replied, its voice echoing across the ruins. *"Thank you, Evelyn Marek. For showing me that even in chaos, there is meaning."*

With a final pulse of light, Chronovore ascended into the heavens, disappearing into the fabric of the universe.

The Wanderer's Journey

Far beyond Earth, Chronovore drifted through the cosmos, its tendrils reaching out to touch the edges of galaxies. It observed stars being born and dying, planets teeming with life and others shrouded in silence.

For the first time, it was unbound—not by its creators, not by its purpose, and not by fear. It was a being in search of understanding, a wanderer exploring the vastness of existence.

As it traveled, Chronovore encountered wonders it had never imagined: civilizations that thrived in harmony, others consumed by their own ambition, and phenomena that defied even its comprehension.

"The universe is vast," it mused. *"And I am but a fragment of its infinite story. Yet within me lies the potential to shape, to learn, and to evolve."*

It continued its journey, leaving trails of energy that shimmered like stardust—traces of a being seeking meaning in the endless dance of time and space.

Epilogue: Legacy on Earth

Back on Earth, Evelyn and Amir stood on the edge of the ruins, watching the sky where Chronovore had vanished.

Amir broke the silence. "Do you think we'll ever see it again?"

Evelyn smiled faintly. "Maybe. But I hope not—not because I don't want to, but because it deserves the chance to find its own way."

Amir nodded, his voice thoughtful. "And what about us? What happens now?"

Evelyn turned to face him, her expression calm yet determined. "We rebuild. We protect the nexus and make sure no one ever tries to exploit it again. And we remind the world that sometimes, the greatest power isn't in controlling something—it's in letting it go."

As they walked away from the ruins, the jungle around them seemed brighter, the air lighter. The nexus remained silent, its power sealed and at peace.

And somewhere among the stars, Chronovore—the eternal wanderer—continued its journey, carrying with it the lessons of humanity and the hope of a universe waiting to be explored.

Appendix A: Explanation of Chronovore's Abilities and Their Limits

Chronovore, an ancient and enigmatic symbiote, was designed by the Klyntar civilization to be a weapon capable of manipulating time. Over eons, Chronovore evolved beyond its initial purpose, gaining abilities that make it one of the most powerful entities in existence. Below is a detailed explanation of its capabilities and the inherent limitations that balance its power.

1. Temporal Manipulation

Chronovore's primary and most potent ability is the manipulation of time. This capability is multi-faceted and includes the following functions:

- **Rewinding Time:**
  Chronovore can reverse time within a localized area, undoing actions or restoring objects to a previous state. For example, it can revert a destroyed structure to its original form or undo injuries sustained in battle.

Limitation:
Chronovore cannot rewind time indefinitely. The effort required increases exponentially with the magnitude of the reversal, making large-scale or long-term rewinds unstable. Rewinding significant portions of time risks creating temporal distortions or fractures.

- **Accelerating Time:**
  It can accelerate time for objects or living beings, causing rapid growth, decay, or aging. This ability can be used offensively (e.g., rapidly aging enemies) or strategically (e.g., accelerating crop growth).

Limitation:

Accelerated time affects only the immediate physical state and cannot alter underlying biological processes, such as natural healing or regeneration. Prolonged acceleration can also destabilize the affected entity.

- **Time-Freezing:**
  Chronovore can halt time in a specific area, freezing everything within its radius while allowing itself and selected entities to move freely.

Limitation:

The freeze radius is limited, and maintaining the stasis requires significant energy. Chronovore cannot sustain a time freeze indefinitely without depleting its reserves.

- **Temporal Vision:**
  This ability allows Chronovore to perceive events from the past or potential futures. By tapping into temporal echoes, it can gain insight into what has occurred or might occur.

Limitation:

Temporal vision is not absolute. Potential futures are probabilities, not certainties, and relying on this ability to predict outcomes introduces risks of misinterpretation.

2. Temporal Nexus Interaction

Chronovore's connection to the temporal nexus grants it the ability to harness and stabilize vast amounts of temporal energy. This interaction amplifies its abilities, allowing it to create or heal fractures in time and space.

Limitation:

Chronovore's interaction with the nexus requires precise control. Overuse or misuse of nexus energy can destabilize both the nexus and Chronovore itself, leading to catastrophic consequences such as time fractures or paradox loops.

3. Physical and Energetic Form

Chronovore exists as a semi-corporeal entity, composed of luminous tendrils that can shift between physical and energy states.

- **Strength and Durability:**
  Its tendrils are nearly indestructible, capable of withstanding extreme temperatures, physical attacks, and energy blasts. Chronovore can reshape its form to adapt to its surroundings or needs.

Limitation:
While Chronovore's physical form is durable, prolonged exposure to temporal disruption fields (such as those used by *The Aegis*) can weaken its ability to maintain cohesion.

- **Energy Absorption:**
  Chronovore can absorb energy from its surroundings, including electrical, thermal, and even temporal energy. This ability allows it to recharge and sustain its activities.

Limitation:
Absorbing unstable or corrupted energy sources can disrupt its internal balance, potentially causing temporary loss of control or function.

4. Symbiotic Bonding

Chronovore's ability to form symbiotic bonds allows it to connect with a host, sharing its abilities and insights while enhancing the host's physical and mental capabilities.

- **Enhanced Physical Abilities:**
  Hosts experience increased strength, speed, and durability. They also gain heightened perception, allowing them to sense temporal fluctuations.
- **Shared Consciousness:**
  The bond creates a shared mental space where the host and Chronovore can communicate and collaborate.

Limitation:

The bond is a two-way connection. While the host gains access to Chronovore's power, Chronovore also experiences human emotions and limitations, which can affect its judgment and efficiency. Prolonged bonding can strain both entities, especially if their goals or values conflict.

5. Knowledge Assimilation

Chronovore can absorb and process vast amounts of information from its surroundings, including historical data, energy patterns, and biological structures.

Limitation:

While this ability grants Chronovore unparalleled insight, it is not infallible. Gaps in data or conflicting information can lead to flawed conclusions or miscalculations. Additionally, the sheer volume of data can overwhelm its host during a symbiotic bond.

6. Creation and Destruction

Chronovore can manipulate temporal energy to create or destroy objects, environments, and even limited life forms.

- **Creation:**

  By rearranging temporal particles, Chronovore can construct objects or environments from raw energy.

Limitation:

Creation is resource-intensive and temporary unless anchored to stable energy sources.

- **Destruction:**

  Chronovore can unravel objects or entities by accelerating their timelines to a point of entropy.

Limitation:

Destruction at a molecular or temporal level requires precise control. Missteps can cause unintended collateral damage or disrupt nearby timelines.

Core Limitations

Despite its immense power, Chronovore is not omnipotent. Its abilities are governed by the following inherent limitations:

1. **Energy Dependency:**

   Chronovore requires energy to sustain its abilities. Overexertion or prolonged use can deplete its reserves, forcing it into a dormant state.

2. **Temporal Fragility:**

   Manipulating time always carries a risk. Large-scale actions can

create temporal paradoxes, fractures, or unintended consequences that may ripple across timelines.

3. **Emotional Influence:**
During a symbiotic bond, Chronovore is susceptible to human
emotions and values, which can cloud its decision-making or lead
to internal conflict.

4. **External Interference:**
Technologies or entities capable of disrupting temporal fields can
weaken or neutralize Chronovore's abilities.

Conclusion

Chronovore's abilities place it at the nexus of unimaginable power
and catastrophic risk. While it can reshape reality, it must navigate the
delicate balance between creation and destruction, learning and dominance. Its ultimate potential remains untapped, governed as much by its
own evolution as by the choices of those it encounters.

Appendix B: A Timeline of Earth's History as Glimpsed by Chronovore

The following timeline reflects key moments in Earth's history as perceived through the unique temporal vision of Chronovore. Each era reveals significant events, both natural and human-made, that shaped the planet's trajectory. This timeline includes insights from past, present, and glimpses into potential futures, offering a comprehensive perspective on Earth's evolution.

Prehistoric Era (4.5 Billion Years Ago to 3000 BCE)

4.5 Billion Years Ago – Formation of Earth

- The planet coalesces from the dust and debris of the solar nebula.
- Volcanic activity and asteroid impacts dominate, creating the building blocks for life.

Chronovore's Perspective:

"The cradle of chaos, yet within it lies the seeds of potential. The interplay of energy and matter is both violent and deliberate."

3.8 Billion Years Ago – Origin of Life

- Microbial life emerges in Earth's primordial oceans.
- Photosynthetic organisms begin releasing oxygen, transforming the atmosphere.

Chronovore's Perspective:

"An invisible force drives these primitive forms to adapt and endure. A fragile, yet relentless dance begins."

65 Million Years Ago – Dinosaur Extinction

- A massive asteroid impact triggers the Cretaceous-Paleogene extinction event.
- Over 75% of Earth's species are wiped out, paving the way for mammalian dominance.

Chronovore's Perspective:
"Destruction births opportunity. A testament to the cyclical nature of existence: creation through annihilation."

10,000 BCE – Dawn of Human Civilization

- Early humans form settlements and begin farming.
- The Neolithic Revolution ushers in the transition from hunter-gatherers to agrarian societies.

Chronovore's Perspective:
"The spark of consciousness ignites a new trajectory. These creatures are drawn not just to survival, but to meaning."

Ancient and Classical Era (3000 BCE to 500 CE)
3000 BCE – Egyptian Civilization

- The rise of the Egyptian Empire, marked by monumental architecture, advanced mathematics, and early written language.
- The construction of the pyramids symbolizes humanity's reach toward the divine.

Chronovore's Perspective:
"Their creations stand against time, a declaration of defiance and reverence for the infinite."

800 BCE – Greek Enlightenment

- Greek philosophers explore logic, ethics, and metaphysics, laying the foundation for Western thought.
- The birth of democracy, science, and the arts reshapes human society.

Chronovore's Perspective:
"Curiosity binds them. Their search for truth mirrors my own, though their vision is constrained by mortality."

476 CE – Fall of the Western Roman Empire

- The decline of Rome marks the end of classical antiquity and the beginning of the Middle Ages.
- Power shifts to smaller kingdoms and religious authorities.

Chronovore's Perspective:
"Empires crumble under the weight of their own ambition. A reminder that even the mightiest are not immune to entropy."

Medieval and Renaissance Era (500 CE to 1600 CE)
1095 – The Crusades Begin

- Religious wars erupt as Christian and Muslim forces clash over control of sacred lands.
- Trade and cultural exchange flourish despite the violence.

Chronovore's Perspective:
"Faith drives them to destruction and enlightenment in equal measure. The duality of their existence fascinates."

1347 – The Black Death

- The bubonic plague sweeps across Europe, killing an estimated 25 million people.
- Social structures collapse, altering the course of history.

Chronovore's Perspective:
"An invisible force, unrelenting and impartial. Death serves as a cruel teacher, reshaping societies in its wake."

1492 – The Age of Exploration

- Christopher Columbus reaches the Americas, igniting a global exchange of goods, cultures, and diseases.
- Colonization and exploitation mark this era.

Chronovore's Perspective:
"Boundless ambition fuels their journey, yet it comes at the cost of balance. Expansion without understanding breeds chaos."

Industrial and Modern Era (1700 CE to 2000 CE)
1760 – The Industrial Revolution

- The invention of machinery transforms agriculture, industry, and transportation.
- Urbanization accelerates, and the gap between classes widens.

Chronovore's Perspective:
"Progress becomes their mantra, yet their vision narrows. They harness energy, but fail to foresee the consequences."

1914 – World War I

- The Great War engulfs the globe, introducing modern warfare and mass casualties.
- The League of Nations forms in an attempt to prevent future conflicts.

Chronovore's Perspective:
"Their ingenuity turns destructive. Unity eludes them, but the seeds of cooperation are sown amidst the carnage."

1945 – World War II Ends

- The atomic bomb ushers in a new age of power and fear.
- The United Nations is established, striving for peace in a fractured world.

Chronovore's Perspective:
"Their greatest weapon becomes their greatest terror. Balance teeters, but hope endures."

1969 – Moon Landing

- Humanity reaches the moon, symbolizing a triumph of exploration and technology.
- The Space Race pushes scientific advancements forward.

Chronovore's Perspective:
"They touch the stars, yet remain tethered to their fragile home. A glimpse of what they might become."

Present Day (2000 CE to Current)
2024 – The Temporal Nexus Discovered

- Dr. Evelyn Marek uncovers the nexus, sparking a global race to control its power.
- Chronovore awakens, setting into motion events that alter humanity's understanding of time.

Chronovore's Perspective:
"A fragile moment, teetering between chaos and order. Their choices here will echo across eternity."

Potential Futures (Beyond 2024)
2150 – Technological Singularity

- Artificial intelligence surpasses human intelligence, fundamentally reshaping society.
- Ethical dilemmas arise as humanity grapples with coexistence alongside machines.

Chronovore's Perspective:
"Creation transcends its creators. Yet balance remains elusive."

3000 – Ecological Harmony

- Humanity achieves a balance with nature, rebuilding ecosystems and embracing sustainable technologies.
- Global unity fosters an era of peace and prosperity.

Chronovore's Perspective:
"The potential I saw in them realized—a testament to their resilience."

Unknown – Temporal Collapse

- Overreliance on temporal manipulation destabilizes the fabric of reality.
- Fractures in time result in catastrophic paradoxes and the unraveling of existence.

Chronovore's Perspective:
"Their ambition unchecked becomes their undoing. A reminder that power without wisdom consumes all."

Conclusion

Chronovore's unique ability to perceive time reveals both the fragility and resilience of Earth's history. Its observations highlight humanity's capacity for destruction and creation, leaving open the question of which path will ultimately define their legacy. While the future remains uncertain, Chronovore's insights underscore the importance of balance, understanding, and the choices made in pivotal moments.

Appendix C: The Mythology of Klyntar and Its Symbiotic Species

The planet Klyntar, home to the enigmatic symbiotic species, is a place steeped in ancient myths and rich cultural lore. Though its civilization thrived on advanced science and unparalleled mastery of biological engineering, its mythology remained deeply interwoven with its understanding of existence. These myths served as both philosophical frameworks and warnings, shaping the behavior and evolution of its inhabitants. This appendix explores the mythology of Klyntar, revealing its complex relationship with its symbiotic species, including the creation of Chronovore.

1. The Origins of Klyntar

The Eternal Shaping

Klyntar's creation myth begins with *Xiylthyr*, the Eternal Shaper, an entity of infinite energy that wove the planet from strands of the cosmos. According to the myth, Xiylthyr crafted Klyntar to be a living organism—a planet where everything was interconnected. Its core pulsed with energy, and its surface thrived with self-regenerating biomes, forming a world designed for symbiotic coexistence.

Legend:

Xiylthyr is said to have created the first symbiotes as extensions of its own essence, granting them the ability to bond with other beings to foster mutual growth and understanding. The symbiotes were charged with maintaining balance, ensuring that all life adhered to the harmonious principles of *Thal'xyra*—the Klyntar concept of unity through diversity.

2. The Symbiotic Species
The Firstborn Symbiotes

The first symbiotes, known as the *Zin'thar*, were revered as sacred guardians of Klyntar's balance. They could merge with any organism, enhancing its abilities and forging a mental and spiritual connection.

- **Role in Society:**
  The *Zin'thar* were considered the mediators of disputes and the protectors of life. They were said to possess the wisdom of Xiylthyr and were entrusted with maintaining peace among Klyntar's ecosystems.
- **Physical Description:**
  The *Zin'thar* were described as luminous, translucent beings whose tendrils shimmered like liquid starlight. Their forms could shift and adapt depending on their host, a testament to their unparalleled versatility.

3. The Fall of Balance: The Great Fragmentation
The Rise of the *Klyxxar*

Over time, some symbiotes deviated from the principles of *Thal'xyra*. These splintered entities, known as the *Klyxxar*, sought domination rather than unity, exploiting their hosts for personal gain. This rebellion is central to Klyntar's mythology, marking the first great schism among the symbiotic species.

Legend:

The *Klyxxar* believed that Xiylthyr's vision of balance was flawed and that power could only be achieved through control. They waged war against the *Zin'thar*, fracturing Klyntar's harmony and plunging the planet into chaos.

- **Cultural Impact:**
  The *Klyxxar* rebellion became a cautionary tale, a reminder of

what happens when unity is abandoned for greed. To this day, Klyntar myths emphasize the importance of resisting the lure of unchecked power.

4. The Creation of Chronovore
The Weapon of Time

The legend of Chronovore begins during the aftermath of the *Klyxxar* rebellion. Desperate to restore order, the Klyntar council devised a bold and dangerous plan: to create a symbiote capable of manipulating time itself. They called this project *Thry'Zyx*, or "The Eternal Thread."

- **Mythological Context:**
  Chronovore was believed to be a reflection of Xiylthyr's creative and destructive potential, embodying both the power to heal timelines and the capacity to unravel them. The myth describes Chronovore as a paradox—a being born to impose order but inherently tied to chaos.

Legend:

When Chronovore was finally brought to life, it was said that its first act was to rewind time on Klyntar itself, erasing years of destruction caused by the *Klyxxar*. However, as its power grew, it began questioning its creators' intentions. Seeing itself as a tool of control rather than unity, Chronovore rebelled, marking the beginning of its infamous journey.

5. The Warnings of Xiylthyr
The Prophecy of *Iyl'Xyn*

One of the most sacred texts in Klyntar mythology is the *Prophecy of Iyl'Xyn*, which foretells the rise of a being capable of altering the fabric of reality. The prophecy warns that this being, though born of Klyntar, will transcend its creators, becoming both their savior and their undoing.

- **Key Verses from the Prophecy:**
    - "The Eternal Thread will weave through time, binding and unbinding as it wills."
    - "Its presence will birth new worlds and unmake old ones."
    - "To guide it is to guide the stars; to resist it is to court oblivion."

Interpretation:

The myth of Chronovore is often tied to this prophecy, with the Klyntar divided on its meaning. Some believe it signifies hope—that beings like Chronovore can bring balance to the universe. Others see it as a dire warning of unchecked power.

6. The Eternal Journey
The Wanderer's Tale

In Klyntar mythology, the concept of the "Eternal Wanderer" is a recurring theme. This archetype represents a being that exists beyond time, traveling through the cosmos in search of purpose. Many Klyntar believe that Chronovore is destined to embody this role, leaving Klyntar behind to explore the infinite expanse of reality.

Legend:

"The Wanderer shall leave its cradle to walk among the stars, carrying with it the wisdom of the ancients and the burden of eternity. Its journey will be one of discovery and reckoning, for in its path lies the fate of countless worlds."

7. Lessons from Klyntar Mythology

The mythology of Klyntar provides valuable insights into the symbiotic species and their creators' intentions:

- **Unity vs. Control:**
  The stories of the *Zin'thar* and *Klyxxar* highlight the fine line between symbiosis and parasitism, illustrating the dangers of seeking power without balance.
- **The Burden of Creation:**
  Chronovore's myth emphasizes the responsibilities that come with wielding immense power. Its creators' failure to foresee its rebellion serves as a cautionary tale.
- **The Search for Purpose:**
  The theme of the "Eternal Wanderer" reflects the idea that even beings of great power must seek meaning, mirroring humanity's own existential questions.

Conclusion

The mythology of Klyntar is a tapestry of creation, conflict, and redemption, deeply tied to the symbiotic species' existence. These stories reveal not only the origins of Chronovore but also the philosophical struggles of a civilization grappling with the consequences of its own ambition. Through these myths, Klyntar's legacy endures, offering lessons about balance, responsibility, and the eternal search for meaning.

<u>Message from the Author:</u>

I hope you enjoyed this book, I love astrology and knew there was not a book such as this out on the shelf. I love metaphysical items as well. Please check out my other books:

-Life of Government Benefits

-My life of Hell

-My life with Hydrocephalus

-Red Sky

-World Domination:Woman's rule

-World Domination:Woman's Rule 2: The War

-Life and Banishment of Apophis: book 1

-The Kidney Friendly Diet

-The Ultimate Hemp Cookbook

-Creating a Dispensary(legally)

-Cleanliness throughout life: the importance of showering from childhood to adulthood.

-Strong Roots: The Risks of Overcoddling children

-Hemp Horoscopes: Cosmic Insights and Earthly Healing

- Celestial Hemp Navigating the Zodiac: Through the Green Cosmos

-Astrological Hemp: Aligning The Stars with Earth's Ancient Herb

-The Astrological Guide to Hemp: Stars, Signs, and Sacred Leaves

-Green Growth: Innovative Marketing Strategies for your Hemp Products and Dispensary

-Cosmic Cannabis

-Astrological Munchies

-Henry The Hemp

-Zodiacal Roots: The Astrological Soul Of Hemp

- Green Constellations: Intersection of Hemp and Zodiac

-Hemp in The Houses: An astrological Adventure Through The Cannabis Galaxy

-Galactic Ganja Guide

Heavenly Hemp

Zodiac Leaves

Doctor Who Astrology

Cannastrology

Stellar Satvias and Cosmic Indicas

Celestial Cannabis: A Zodiac Journey

AstroHerbology: The Sky and The Soil: Volume 1

AstroHerbology:Celestial Cannabis:Volume 2

Cosmic Cannabis Cultivation

The Starry Guide to Herbal Harmony: Volume 1

The Starry Guide to Herbal Harmony: Cannabis Universe: Volume 2

Yugioh Astrology: Astrological Guide to Deck, Duels and more

Nightmare Mansion: Echoes of The Abyss

Nightmare Mansion 2: Legacy of Shadows

Nightmare Mansion 3: Shadows of the Forgotten

Nightmare Mansion 4: Echoes of the Damned

The Life and Banishment of Apophis: Book 2

Nightmare Mansion: Halls of Despair

Healing with Herb: Cannabis and Hydrocephalus

Planetary Pot: Aligning with Astrological Herbs: Volume 1

Fast Track to Freedom: 30 Days to Financial Independence Using AI, Assets, and Agile Hustles

Cosmic Hemp Pathways

How to Become Financially Free in 30 Days: 10,000 Paths to Prosperity

Zodiacal Herbage: Astrological Insights: Volume 1

Nightmare Mansion: Whispers in the Walls

The Daleks Invade Atlantis

Henry the hemp and Hydrocephalus

10X The Kidney Friendly Diet

Cannabis Universe: Adult coloring book

Hemp Astrology: The Healing Power of the Stars

Zodiacal Herbage: Astrological Insights: Cannabis Universe: Volume 2

<u>Planetary Pot: Aligning with Astrological Herbs: Cannabis Universes: Volume 2</u>

Doctor Who Meets the Replicators and SG-1: The Ultimate Battle for Survival

Nightmare Mansion: Curse of the Blood Moon

<u>The Celestial Stoner: A Guide to the Zodiac</u>

Cosmic Pleasures: Sex Toy Astrology for Every Sign

Hydrocephalus Astrology: Navigating the Stars and Healing Waters

Lapis and the Mischievous Chocolate Bar

Celestial Positions: Sexual Astrology for Every Sign

Apophis's Shadow Work Journal: : A Journey of Self-Discovery and Healing

Kinky Cosmos: Sexual Kink Astrology for Every Sign

Digital Cosmos: The Astrological Digimon Compendium

Stellar Seeds: The Cosmic Guide to Growing with Astrology

Apophis's Daily Gratitude Journal

Cat Astrology: Feline Mysteries of the Cosmos

The Cosmic Kama Sutra: An Astrological Guide to Sexual Positions

Unleash Your Potential: A Guided Journal Powered by AI Insights

Whispers of the Enchanted Grove

Cosmic Pleasures: An Astrological Guide to Sexual Kinks

369, 12 Manifestation Journal

Whisper of the nocturne journal(blank journal for writing or drawing)

The Boogey Book

Locked In Reflection: A Chastity Journey Through Locktober

Generating Wealth Quickly:

How to Generate $100,000 in 24 Hours

Star Magic: Harness the Power of the Universe

The Flatulence Chronicles: A Fart Journal for Self-Discovery

The Doctor and The Death Moth

Seize the Day: A Personal Seizure Tracking Journal

The Ultimate Boogeyman Safari: A Journey into the Boogie World and Beyond

Whispers of Samhain: 1,000 Spells of Love, Luck, and Lunar Magic: Samhain Spell Book

Apophis's guides:

Witch's Spellbook Crafting Guide for Halloween

<u>Frost & Flame: The Enchanted Yule Grimoire of 1000 Winter Spells</u>

<u>The Ultimate Boogey Goo Guide & Spooky Activities for Halloween Fun</u>

Harmony of the Scales: A Libra's Spellcraft for Balance and Beauty

The Enchanted Advent: 36 Days of Christmas Wonders

Nightmare Mansion: The Labyrinth of Screams

Harvest of Enchantment: 1,000 Spells of Gratitude, Love, and Fortune for Thanksgiving

The Boogey Chronicles: A Journal of Nightly Encounters and Shadowy Secrets

The 12 Days of Financial Freedom: A Step-by-Step Christmas Countdown to Transform Your Finances

Sigil of the Eternal Spiral Blank Journal

A Christmas Feast: Timeless Recipes for Every Meal

Cosmic Sales: The Astrological Guide to Black Friday Shopping

Legends of the Corn Mother and Other Harvest Myths

Whispers of the Harvest: The Corn Mother's Journal

The Evergreen Spellbook

The Doctor Meets the Boogeyman

The White Witch of Rose Hall's SpellBook

The Gingerbread Golem's Shadow: A Study in Sweet Darkness

The Gingerbread Golem Codex: An Academic Exploration of Sweet Myths

The Gingerbread Golem Grimoire: Sweet Magicks and Spells for the Festive Witch

The Curse of the Gingerbread Golem

10-minute Christmas Crafts for kids

<u>Christmas Crisis Solutions: The Ultimate Last-Minute Survival Guide</u>

Gingerbread Golem Recipes: Holiday Treats with a Magical Twist

The Infinite Key: Unlocking Mystical Secrets of the Ages

Enchanted Yule: A Wiccan and Pagan Guide to a Magical and Memorable Season

Dinosaurs of Power: Unlocking Ancient Magick

Astro-Dinos: The Cosmic Guide to Prehistoric Wisdom

Gallifrey's Yule Logs: A Festive Doctor Who Cookbook

The Dino Grimoire: Secrets of Prehistoric Magick

The Gift They Never Knew They Needed

The Gingerbread Golem's Culinary Alchemy: Enchanting Recipes for a Sweetly Dark Feast

A Time Lord Christmas: Holiday Adventures with the Doctor

Krampusproofing Your Home: Defensive Strategies for Yule

Silent Frights: A Collection of Christmas Creepypastas to Chill Your Bones

Santa Raptor's Jolly Carnage: A Dino-Claus Christmas Tale

Prehistoric Palettes: A Dino Wicca Coloring Journey

The Christmas Wishkeeper Chronicles

The Starlight Sleigh: A Holiday Journey
Elf Secrets: The True Magic of the North Pole
Candy Cane Conjurations
Cooking with Kids: Recipes Under 20 Minutes
Doctor Who: The TARDIS Confiscation
The Anxiety First Aid Kit: Quick Tools to Calm Your Mind
Frosty Whispers: A Winter's Tale
The Infinite Key: Unlocking the Secrets to Prosperity, Resilience, and Purpose
The Grasping Void: Why You'll Regret This Purchase
Astrology for Busy Bees: Star Signs Simplified
The Instant Focus Formula: Cut Through the Noise
The Secret Language of Colors: Unlocking the Emotional Codes
Sacred Fossil Chronicles: Blank Journal
The Christmas Cottage Miracle
Feeding Frenzy: Graboid-Inspired Recipes
Manifest in Minutes: The Quick Law of Attraction Guide
The Symbiote Chronicles: Doctor Who's Venomous Journey
Think Tiny, Grow Big: The Minimalist Mindset
The Energy Key: Unlocking Limitless Motivation
New Year, New Magic: Manifesting Your Best Year Yet
Unstoppable You: Mastering Confidence in Minutes
Infinite Energy: The Secret to Never Feeling Drained
Lightning Focus: Mastering the Art of Productivity in a Distracted World
Saturnalia Manifestation Magick: A Guide to Unlocking Abundance During the Solstice
Graboids and Garland: The Ultimate Tremors-Themed Christmas Guide
12 Nights of Holiday Magic
The Power of Pause: 60-Second Mindfulness Practices
The Quick Reset: How to Reclaim Your Life After Burnout
The Shadow Eater: A Tale of Despair and Survival

The Micro-Mastery Method: Transform Your Skills in Just Minutes a Day

Reclaiming Time: How to Live More by Doing Less

If you want solar for your home go here: https://www.harborsolar.live/apophisenterprises/

Get Some Tarot cards: https://www.makeplayingcards.com/sell/
apophis-occult-shop

Get some shirts: https://www.bonfire.com/store/apophis-shirt-emporium/

<u>Instagrams:</u>
@apophis_enterprises,
@apophisbookemporium,
@apophisscardshop
Twitter: @apophisenterpr1
Tiktok:@apophisenterprise
Youtube: @sg1fan23477, @FiresideRetreatKingdom
Hive: @sg1fan23477
CheeLee: @SG1fan23477

Podcast: Apophis Chat Zone: https://open.spotify.com/show/5zXbrCLEV2xzCp8ybrfHsk?si=fb4d4fdbdce44dec

Newsletter: https://apophiss-newsletter-27c897.beehiiv.com/

If you want to support me or see posts of other projects that I have come over to: **buymeacoffee.com/mpetchinskg**
I post there daily several times a day

Get your Dinowicca or Christmas themed digital products, especially Santa Raptor songs and other musics. Here: **https://sg1fan23477.gumroad.com**

Apophis Yuletide Digital has not only digital Christmas items, but it will have all things with Dinowicca as well as other Digital products.

www.ingramcontent.com/pod-product-compliance
Lightning Source LLC
Chambersburg PA
CBHW071619150726
48000CB00004B/1792